This Time, She Wasn't Going To Overreact And Imagine A Mountain Out Of A Simple, Single Kiss.

If her heart was racing and her knees feeling shakier than limp noodles, there was a logical reason for it. And as an experienced coward, she had a predictable allergic reaction to anything dangerous.

If she went with Steve to see the pups, she risked a confrontation with the adult wolves in that pack again. But his wolf cubs *were* irresistible. Something about those cubs made her maternal instincts go turbo—she was crazy about the little guys.

That reaction, she told herself, had nothing to do with seeing *Steve* again.

It was the wolves she was worried about.

Not him.

Dear Reader,

This month it seems like everyone's in romantic trouble. We have runaway brides and jilted grooms....They've been left at the altar and wonder if they'll *ever* find true love with the right person.

Of course they do, and we get to find out how, as we read Silhouette Desire's delightful month of "Jilted!" heroes and heroines.

And what better way to start this special month than with *The Accidental Bridegroom,* a second 1994 *Man of the Month* from one of your favorites, Ann Major? I'm sure you'll enjoy this passionate story of seduction and supposed betrayal as much as I do.

And look for five more fabulous books by some of your most beloved writers: Dixie Browning, Cait London, Raye Morgan, Jennifer Greene and Cathie Linz. Yes, their characters might have been left at the altar...but they don't stay single for long!

So don't pick and choose—read about them all! I loved these stories, and I'm sure you will, too.

Lucia Macro
Senior Editor

Please address questions and book requests to:
Silhouette Reader Service
U.S.: 3010 Walden Ave., P.O. Box 1325, Buffalo, NY 14269
Canadian: P.O. Box 609, Fort Erie, Ont. L2A 5X3

JENNIFER GREENE
A GROOM FOR
RED RIDING HOOD

Ingram 11/8/94 $2.99

SILHOUETTE *Desire*®
Published by Silhouette Books
America's Publisher of Contemporary Romance

107691

SILHOUETTE BOOKS

ISBN 0-373-05893-4

A GROOM FOR RED RIDING HOOD

Books by Jennifer Greene

Silhouette Desire

Body and Soul #263
Foolish Pleasure #293
Madam's Room #326
Dear Reader #350
Minx #366
Lady Be Good #385
Love Potion #421
The Castle Keep #439
Lady of the Island #463
Night of the Hunter #481
Dancing in the Dark #498
Heat Wave #553
Slow Dance #600
Night Light #619
Falconer #671
Just Like Old Times #728
It Had To Be You #756
Quicksand #786
Bewitched #847
Bothered #855
Bewildered #861
A Groom for Red Riding Hood #893

*Jock's Boys

Silhouette Intimate Moments

Secrets #221
Devil's Night #305
Broken Blossom #345
Pink Topaz #418

Silhouette Books

Birds, Bees and Babies 1990
"Riley's Baby"

JENNIFER GREENE

lives near Lake Michigan with her husband and two children. Before writing full-time, she worked as a teacher and personnel manager. Michigan State University honored her as an "outstanding woman graduate" for her work with women on campus.

Ms. Greene has written more than forty category romances, for which she has won numerous awards, including the RITA for Best Short Contemporary Book, and both a Best Series Author and a Lifetime Achievement award from *Romantic Times*.

Prologue

Mary Ellen Barnett slammed the car door, hitched her wedding gown to her knees and hiked up the porch steps into the kitchen. Without a pause for breath, she locked the door, pulled the curtains, flipped open the oven and switched on the gas.

Suicide was for cowards, but that didn't bother her—she'd been an ace pro coward for years. Truthfully, she was feeling more murderous than suicidal, but that was irrelevant, too. She'd had it. Really had it. Being jilted at the altar wasn't the first time she'd made a humiliating fool of herself, but it was positively the last.

The sickly sweet gas fumes invaded the small, closed kitchen quickly. Too quickly. Cripes, they were making her gag. She'd never manage to kill herself off—at least not before throwing up.

Impatiently she jerked off the gas, snapped the oven door closed and stormed outside.

There had to be another way. Yanking off her long white veil, she plopped her fanny on the porch steps and inhaled gulping lungfuls of fresh air.

A balmy breeze drifted off the Georgia coast. The blasted evening was damn near breathtaking. In any normal Christmas season, the weather would be obligingly cold, damp and dreary. Not this year. The wind drifted through her hair, as soothing as a caress, as soft as a whisper. The stars were just coming out, backdropped against a velvet sky and a dreamer's crescent moon.

The night was so disgustingly wonderful that it was darn near impossible to concentrate on doing herself in, but Mary Ellen was furiously, stubbornly, bull-dog-determined. How many times had she made embarrassing, mortifying, humiliating mistakes? Millions, that's how many. The flaws in her character were unfixable. God knew, she'd tried. And though her self-esteem and self-respect were nonexistent at the moment, she'd never lacked for imagination. The trick was simply applying her fertile mind to effective suicide methods.

She stuck her chin in her palm. Minutes passed. As violently and tenaciously as she focused on morbid thoughts...self-destructing just wasn't going to be that easy.

Gas was out. Car crashes were no good, either—there was too much risk of hurting someone else; she'd die before hurting anyone else—and if she screwed up and failed to take herself out, she could end up a vegetable on machines that someone had to take care of. That was out of the question. Hanging was even less palatable—somebody would be stuck finding a gruesome scene. The time-honored traditional method of slitting one's wrists had that same unfortunate glitch and anyway she hated—*really* hated—the sight of blood.

She concentrated harder.

Poison struck her as a stupendous idea, but the thought of drinking drain cleaner was too repulsive to stomach. Swallowing enough pills to go to sleep was the easiest out, but there was an inherent problem with that method, too. She'd always been as healthy as a horse. The only medicine laying around was a little PMS stuff, and since that was a regular plague, there were only a few pills left in the bottle. Somehow she didn't think taking six tablets was going to get the job done.

Drowning was a possibility, but awfully tough to pull off. She could swim like a fish. Starvation? Mary Ellen rolled her eyes to the sky. That'd *never* work. She'd been born with the appetite of a lumberjack. If there was food around, for absolute sure, she'd never have the self-control to turn it down.

She scowled. There *had* to be some way. A suicide method that she couldn't bungle. A way that left no mess and looked like an accident—everyone in town knew she was distraught and distracted after that debacle tonight in the church, so a careless accident would be understandable. She didn't want anyone blaming themselves. She'd never deliberately hurt anyone.

But damnation, there didn't seem to be a method that fit all the criteria.

The more she thought about it, the more she came to the unavoidably nasty conclusion that—blast and hell!—she was just going to have to live.

That morose thought barely registered before an alternative took its place. She could run. If she was cowardly enough to consider suicide—which she certainly was—there was certainly no reason to sweat any scruples about running away from her problems. No one would miss her. Like removing a thorn or a bee stinger, it would be a relief to everyone if she were gone. She'd been a Class A problem from the day she was born, especially for those she loved. And living down this latest fiasco and humiliation would be far easier if she were removed from the picture.

The idea of running gained momentum like a tumbleweed gathering speed in a high wind. She could do it. Disappear. Become someone else. Go someplace where no one knew her or had any idea what a disastrous mess she'd made of her life.

Positively it had to be a place with no men—she'd made a fool of herself for absolutely the last time over *that* half of the human species—but that tiny detail presented more of a challenge than a problem. There had to be someplace in the continental United States that had no men.

She just had to find it.

One

Steve Rawlings pushed open the door to Samson's and stomped the snow off his boots. The sudden warmth and light made his eyes sting. He yanked off his gloves and hat and automatically headed for the far booth in back. As he expected, the bit of a bar was packed. There was nothing to do on a bitter, blizzardy Monday night in Eagle Falls—except drink and indulge in a little male bonding over a football game.

The Lions were playing on the black-and-white over the bar. The picture was fuzzy—TV reception was typically nip and tuck in this isolated corner of Michigan's Upper Peninsula. Also, typically, beer was flowing freely. A few heads turned when Steve walked by. None of the men nodded or asked him to pull up a chair. He'd probably have keeled over from shock if they did. His work automatically gave him the popularity of a piranha with an infectious disease. He was used to it. So far, the guys had given him a wide, wary berth, but there were no overt signs of hostility. Hell, he'd been some places where people greeted him with a shotgun.

Blowing on his cold hands, he slid into the worn pine booth. The windchill factor was a mean subzero. He'd been working outside for the better part of six hours. His boots were caked with ice, his hands too numb to function and his stomach was growling with hunger. Stiffly he unzipped his parka and pushed the coat off his shoulders. His head was bent when he heard the soft, feminine magnolia drawl. His eyes shot up.

There were women in Eagle Falls. Just not many. The total local population couldn't be more than a few hundred—summer cottages and hunting cabins were all boarded up by this time of year, and even the timber industry shut down in the dead of winter. Permanent residents were few. The area attracted wilderness lovers, loners, and for sure some families, but mostly people who chose to march to a different drummer. There were no lone women, for the obvious reason that there was spit little to appeal to a woman alone.

And especially a young woman like her.

She stood out like a rose in a pen of bulls. There wasn't a line on her face—she couldn't be thirty—and wearing boots, she stood maybe five foot six. A cap of glossy hair framed her face, mink brown, worn short and smooth. Classic beauty was the wrong label. Cute was more like it. Real cute, honest cute. Her nose had a sassy tip, her chin had a dimple and a slash of dark brows arched over huge, startling blue eyes. Her mouth was small, naked of lipstick, as pink as a petal and shaped like a bow.

Steve rubbed the circulation back into his cold hands, studying the rest of her. Her clothes were straight L.L. Bean, a flapping flannel shirt worn over a black turtleneck sweater and jeans. The clothes looked new, the jeans still stiff, her boots unscuffed. Still, the denim fabric faithfully cupped the curve of a truly delectable fanny, and a man would have to be both blind and brain-dead *not* to notice how unforgettably she filled out that turtleneck.

He couldn't imagine what she was doing here.

Samson, the owner of the bar, was getting up in years and was plagued with arthritis. Steve understood why the old codger had hired help, just not how she fit in. Conceivably she'd waited tables and tended bar before, but he doubted it. Frowning, he watched her awkwardly handling a heavy tray. Her clumsy juggling of the beer mugs suggested a total lack of experience at the job.

When her hands were full, Fred Claire took advantage and patted her behind with a wink for the other guys. Brick red color skated up her cheeks. A mug of beer started to tip and spill. The tray clattered to the table.

Steve scratched his chin. He had a sixth sense for trouble. Honing and fine-tuning that instinct was an automatic requirement with his work. In this case, he didn't smell trouble. Nothing about her attire was deliberately suggestive, but if she thought she could escape the guys' attention in this place, she had to have a dreamer's fantasy life. Most of the men were middle-aged, a fair slug of them married—hardly Lothario types, but hell, she was a testosterone-arousing package of new, young, female and good-looking. The boys giving her a rush was as predictable as conflict in the Middle East.

Rowdy laughter echoed from the crowded table by the door. Fred and his cronies had clearly been drinking for several hours now, and they were all making a teasing fuss over the spilled beer. Rafer claimed loudly that there was a wet spot in his lap that he'd sure appreciate her helping him with. The others snickered at his wit. The splotches of color on her cheeks darkened to the hue of a raw burn.

She was still flustered when she glanced up and spotted him. As soon as she escaped that table, she headed over and flipped open her order pad. "I'm sorry you had to wait. What would you like?"

"Coffee. And a couple of steaks if Samson's still got any in back. Rare."

She scribbled the order with her head tucked down, paying no attention to him until she suddenly glanced up. "A couple of steaks?" she echoed.

"A couple. As in two," he affirmed.

She looked at him then. With him sitting down, she had no way of knowing he was six-three, but her gaze flickered over his rangy frame and broad shoulders. She wasn't the first woman to check him over. It wasn't Steve's fault he was a hard man to ignore—he had no vote in his genetic inheritance—but his height and linebacker build made it tricky to hide in a crowd. His jet black hair, blue eyes and ruddy, clear skin added up to striking looks that had an embarrassing habit of attracting female attention. Most women took a second look.

Not her. After that quick shot at his face and shoulder span, her eyes dropped. Fast. She promptly wrote down "two" and underlined it. "I can see it'll be an uphill job filling you up. I'll nuke a couple of potatoes. And I think there's still a piece of apple pie in back—"

"That'd be great."

"You want your coffee black or with cream?"

"Black'll do."

"Okay. I'll be back as quick as I can."

She spun around, not once looking at him again—but he'd had more than enough time to do a prowling close-up of her. Once the flush climbed down from her cheeks, her skin was as pale as ivory. Her voice was a velvet Southern drawl, soft, feminine and as vulnerable as everything else about her. The tag on her shirt read "Mary Ellen." If Mary Ellen was looking for men, she'd positively picked the right place. Winters were long and lonesome in this neck of the woods, and she couldn't find a higher male-to-female ratio outside of Alaska. Still, the image of man hungry didn't work at all. Her posture was as stiff as a poker, her expression a mirror of nerves and wariness, and those incredible eyes of hers were as skittish as a newborn colt's.

He watched her take another order—standing as she had at his booth, careful to keep from pinching and patting distance, not looking any of the boys in the eye—and then she disappeared into the back. A masculine bellow echoed through the room when the Lions fumbled the ball. Samson shot out from the kitchen, his white hair standing in spikes, waving a spatula, to armchair coach with the rest of them.

Steve rolled his shoulders, mentally blocking out the football game and the noise and his curiosity about the waitress, too. She wasn't his problem. Heaven knew, he had problems of his own. The smoky warmth of the bar was slowly unthawing his frozen bones, and weariness was starting to hit him in waves. If his stomach hadn't been pit-empty, he'd have driven straight to his trailer and six straight hours in bed. His body was used to being pushed, and this snow squall was no worse than a hundred he'd seen growing up on a Wyoming ranch, but the cold and exhaustion combined had been killers today. Weariness was dogging him as relentlessly as a shadow.

He didn't know his eyes had closed, yet they must have, because the aroma of fresh coffee suddenly startled him. The steaming mug was sitting in front of him, hotter than the devil's breath. Mary Ellen had come and gone without his hearing her, but he could see her now, dodging around the room, serving fresh pitchers of foaming beer, ducking under the TV so she didn't block the view. Someone called out, "Sweetheart? Darlin', we desperately need you over here." He saw her jaw clench and that cherry color shoot to her cheeks again.

If there was a woman less suited to working in a bar, he couldn't imagine one.

Over the next hour, she came to his table three times. She never said a word, never looked at him, but she kept his coffee filled; she served his steaks blood-rare with potatoes and trimmings he'd never asked for, noticed when he'd leveled that, and came back with a fat slice of apple pie heaped with ice cream. She didn't hover—hell, she didn't even ask what he wanted—but she took better care of him than a mother hen.

Steve couldn't help but notice that her quiet competence around him was a direct contrast to her behavior around the other men. He'd always had a gift with wild critters—animals instinctively trusted him.

But women were a distinctly different species. The lady didn't need any great perceptive skills to realize that the other men treated him like a pariah. For most women, that would be a steer-clear clue that he was a man to be avoided, and with his height and size, the last instinct he usually aroused in females was security. Yet she treated him as if she'd instantly labeled him "safe," no one who was going to cause her trouble. Although that was certainly true, it made her behavior around the other guys downright bewildering.

He wolfed down a bite of pie, watching Fred Claire try to cop another feel. A bowl of peanuts skittered when Mary Ellen jerked back.

Steve forced his attention on the pie. Samson's specialty was apple pie; the apples were heavy on the nutmeg and cinnamon, not too much sugar, the crust as flaky as his own mother's. Delicious. No reason at all for a lump to lodge in his throat. There was nothing going on at that far corner table by the door that he needed to think or worry about.

He wasn't bosom buddies with Fred—or anyone else in Eagle Falls—but those particular people were regulars at the bar. He'd seen them often enough to have their measure. Fred's brush cut was clipped shorter than a marine's; he favored dressing in army fatigues, playing weekend war games, flashing a lot of weapons and coaxing anyone who'd listen into talking about his conspiracy theories. Maybe he wasn't the average Joe, but basically he was harmless, a lot of big talk but no action.

A raucous snicker of masculine laughter echoed across the room.

Steve didn't lift his head. She wasn't really in trouble. There wasn't anything tricky or difficult about handling Fred. Either a smile or a scolding would have put him—or any of the boys—in their place. By taking their teasing so seriously, it was the same as begging for more. Any woman who had an older brother or chose to work around men would surely know that. The boys had had too much beer. They were feeling their hormones. Nobody was going to ignore her if she kept rising to the bait.

He was on the last bite of pie when she whisked over and slipped the bill under his plate. She'd bitten her bottom lip a bruised red. The look around her eyes was pinched and drawn. Still, her magnolia drawl had a winsome shyness. "I'll be back if y'all need change," she said.

She'd already moved on before Steve had the chance to dig into his back pocket for his wallet. Change was no problem. He smacked the bills on the table, more than enough to include a walloping tip—which she'd earned. That easily, he told himself, she was completely off his mind. All his attention was focused on getting home. Already he could picture the double bed in his trailer, slipping between the sheets buck naked, burrowing into the warmth of a down comforter. Nothing was quieter than a night in the north woods, and the hot meal had pushed him over an edge. He was dizzy-tired, gut-tired, darn near mean-tired.

He could have sworn he wasn't still watching her. Yet when he reached back for his parka, his eyes seemed to be peeled across the room, because he saw the exact moment when Fred hooked an arm around her waist.

She wasn't carrying a tray that time, but she wasn't expecting the pass, either. She landed with an awkward plop in Fred Claire's lap. Fred said something—

undoubtedly some kind of vulgar compliment, because it made the other men guffaw. She was trying to scramble off him. Fred was trying to keep her pinned.

Steve muttered an exasperated "Hell" under his breath and lurched to his feet. He didn't need this. He had troubles of his own, and getting along with the good old boys in town was integral to resolving those troubles. But dammit, her face wasn't flushed this time. It was stark white. Even from yards away, he could see her expression wasn't just flustered or embarrassed, but downright, outright scared.

He stalked over, his step so quiet that no one even realized he was there—until he reached over and plucked the lady off Fred's lap.

"Hey," Fred objected.

It took a second to steady her. For that instant his hands were on her waist, he felt the supple warmth of her body and caught the vague drift of a subtle, feminine scent. His libido stirred, with a punch of sexual awareness that he'd never expected—but it didn't last long.

"Hey!" Fred snarled again, nearly tipping the table when he jerked out of his chair.

Steve had no time to release an aggrieved masculine sigh. No question, when a man asked for trouble, he got it. Fred had been drinking for how many hours? His leathery face had a beer flush and the adrenaline of rage was flashing in his eyes. Steve grasped him by the shirt collar, quick. "I'm going to worry about you driving home after all that drinking," he said calmly. "Wouldn't you say that a good friend would help you sober up?"

Chairs scraped across the plank floor. As if a bomb had dropped, there was suddenly no sound in the room except for the blare of the Lion's announcer on the boob tube. No one attempted to get in the way as Steve propelled Fred toward the door. There was no reason for anyone to object. It was the best entertainment anyone had enjoyed that night—short of watching one small woman get picked on.

The wind had finally died, but the air was colder than a witch's heart when Steve yanked open the door. The icy air slammed straight into his lungs. It was dark out, but the fresh foot of snow had the sharp, bright gleam of sequins. He released Fred's collar, bent down, scooped up a handful of snow and washed Fred's face with it. His intuition was correct. The method helped Fred sober up right quick. The other man threw a punch. He got his face washed a second time for that asinine move.

"Where I come from, a man doesn't pick on someone smaller than him. Only bullies do that, and I never met a bully yet who wasn't a coward. Now, you got that message, or you want to discuss it a little while longer?"

Apparently Fred was in the mood for an in-depth discussion, although the subject of bullies never came up again. He let loose a string of four-letter words, including extensive commentary about Steve's mother, her preference for combat boots and the shaky sexual preferences of his father. He didn't throw another punch, though.

"Look, you're drunk," Steve said quietly. "Damn stupid to fight when you're drunk. When you sober up, if you're still looking for a fight, you come pick on me. I'll take you on, if that's what you really want. Just leave the lady alone, you hear me?"

Fred seemed to feel that comment required another wordy dissertation on his character, values and manhood—or lack thereof. It took an enormous amount of wind and hot air before he ran out of insults. Steve listened patiently the whole time. The Japanese had always understood that once a man lost face, he became an enemy. No man forgot being humiliated. Steve let him get the last word in for the same reason he hadn't leveled the little hothead in front of his cronies inside. He wasn't looking to make an enemy out of Fred Claire—or anyone else in Eagle Falls. He just wanted Ms. Blue Eyes left alone.

Once Fred's windup insults ran down, Steve waited, studying his face. The begging-to-fight fire was dying in his eyes, the adrenaline settling back down. Fred was just plain cold, shivering violently in his shirt-sleeves, snow dripping from his face and down his neck. A few minutes in subzero temperatures had a way of equalizing everything, even challenged male egos and bad tempers. Fred was no longer having fun.

Steve took one last look at his face. And walked away.

Men. Since the only thing Mary Ellen wanted to avoid was that particular half of the human species, it seemed the height of irony that she'd landed in a nest of the vipers. Of course, her specialty was screwing up. She never made small mistakes. Her forte had always been the big, classic, mortifyingly embarrassing-type boners.

She stuffed her hair under a stocking cap and grabbed her ski poles. Inhaling a lungful of crisp clean air, she reassured herself that moving here had been the best thing that ever happened to her. True, she'd misjudged the population of men. Equally true, she'd failed to consider the teensy problem of money. In her wildest nightmare she'd never anticipated having to work in a bar, but there'd simply been no other job around.

Still, her shift at Samson's didn't start until four in the afternoon. Her day was free until then. All her day hours were free.

She pushed off, her cross-country skis forging a fresh track in the new snow. Wonders surrounded her. Raised in the South, she'd never dreamed of snow like this. The rolling pine woods were deep, peaceful, quiet. Where sunlight shot down, the new snow laid on the emerald branches like a white satin glaze. A scarlet cardinal caught her eye. A soft-furred bunny scampered across her path.

She didn't know where she was going. Didn't care. She hadn't misjudged how soul renewing this isolated area would be. There were endless acres of woods and wilderness to explore. Her rented cabin was an idyllic retreat for a woman planning to live as a hermitmonkess. There was no family around for her to disappoint. No town looking over her shoulder, waiting for her next I-told-you-so screwup. And although the Freds and the Georges and the Ben McCreries were giving her fits at the bar, during the day she didn't have to even see a human being with a Y chromosome unless she wanted to. And there was positively no man appealing enough to tempt her aggravatingly impulsive heart.

An image of a giant with searing blue eyes drifted through her mind.

She let the image linger, simply because there was no harm, no possible temptation involved. She remembered the stranger's overwhelming height, the impact of his startling eyes. She remembered thinking that he was an incredible hunk, and for the same reason feeling a rare sensation of being safe. Hunks never preyed on her. Her looks were too ordinary.

And for once, her first judgment of a man had been accurate. The whole time she waited on him, he'd been kind and quiet, but there'd been no teasing or come-ons. He just wasn't the kind of man who would ever be interested in her. Looking at him was like indulging in window-shopping at a candy store when the door was locked. There was no threat of her suckering into those dangerous calories. His face was square cut, strong boned, ruggedly handsome; there was character in the etched lines around his eyes and mouth. She wasn't likely to forget it.

Nor had she forgotten the way he'd suddenly gotten up and hustled Fred Claire outside. At the time, it barely registered that he was rescuing her. He'd moved like a hunter, swift and sure, hauling Fred outside faster than anyone knew what was happening. He'd never said anything, never came back in. Mary Ellen still didn't know what he'd done, but when Mr. Jerk returned to his table, he'd been as polite as a Catholic schoolboy and he'd pointedly ignored her for the last three nights now.

She owed that giant big time.

He'd get his thanks—if she ever saw him again—but right now she had other things on her mind. Her skis hissed through the new-fallen snow. She was still new to the sport, still prone to an occasional clumsy tumble, but getting better. As she worked up a rhythm, the crisp air pinkened her cheeks and stung her eyes.

Every day she trekked farther and explored new directions. She'd been so crushed when she first moved here. Occasionally she still thought about Johnny. Occasionally she still woke up in a cold sweat, reliving the nightmare of a bride in a white dress, standing in the church for a Christmas Eve wedding, the guests all there, the whole town waiting for a groom who never showed.

That humiliating memory still made her cringe, but she'd slowly realized that that singular rejection wasn't the real source of her hurt. It was being wrong, one too many times. It was feeling, once too often, the stone weight of being unloved and unlovable. Johnny had turned out to be a turkey, but Johnny wasn't the real problem. Her self-respect was in more crumpled pieces than a broken cookie.

That cookie refused to instantly glue back together—but she was working on it.

When she brushed against a pine branch, snow shivered down in a shower of fluffy crystals, making her chuckle. It wasn't so hard, being happy. It wasn't so impossible, to laugh again. Being alive was riches enough, and she was discovering more riches every day.

She poled to the crest of a hill, and then, bending her knees, sailed down to the belly of a small valley. At the bottom she stopped, breathless and exhilarated, and yanked off a glove to check the compass in her pocket. Northeast. If she kept going in that direction, eventually she'd hit Lake Superior. Even if the landscape was totally unfamiliar, she had her bearings, wasn't afraid of being lost. She zipped the compass back into her jacket pocket again, and was just refitting her glove when she saw the animal.

Fear never occurred to her in that first instant. He looked like a dog. A Siberian-husky type. He had a long snout and pointy ears, and mesmerizingly liquid black eyes staring right at her. His luxuriously thick pelt was almost as stark white as the snow. Her eyes softened. Lord, he was gorgeous, and standing motionless from a knoll thirty feet from her, as regal and silent as a statue.

"Hey, boy," she said softly. "Are you lost?"

Her tone was as gentle as a whisper—she'd fallen in love on sight—but his response to her was distinctly different. At the first sound of her voice, he bared huge pointed teeth and snarled, his growl so ferocious that her throat closed.

It wasn't a dog. She knew it in a pulsebeat. No husky was that big; no tame animal made wild, feral sounds like that. It had to be a wolf.

Every muscle in her body clenched up and locked. She couldn't swallow. Adrenaline shot through her veins in an ice-cold rush.

The wolf paced another five feet closer, snapping threatening growls the whole time. It wasn't hard to get the message. He didn't like her. She'd have been thrilled to turn tail and run, only damned if she wasn't too scared to move. She heard another snarl and whipped her head around.

Another one. Lord. Another two—no, three. At least three of them. The others were multicolored, their pelts ranging from dark charcoal to streaky gray. None of them were as huge as the white wolf, but the few pounds difference was hardly reassuring. She sensed as well as saw that she was being circled. They were moving. Pacing slowly in the snow, ducking in and behind trees, but keeping her in sight.

She'd have wet her pants if she had time.

There was no time. Panic sealed her throat. She had a flash memory of the afternoon she'd idiotically considered suicide. She'd never meant it. She'd just been so angry with herself—being stood up at her wedding had been a last straw in a long history of humiliating, embarrassing screwups. But geesh. At her most stupid, she'd never really wanted to die. And for sure she didn't want to die all alone, torn to shreds in the middle of the north woods by a pack of wolves.

It was positively an uphill, difficult and darn near insurmountable job to earn her own self-respect. But she wanted a chance. *Come on, God. I'm trying so hard, but I need a little time. How about a bargain. You get me out of this, and I'll never mess up again as long as I live. I'll be so good you'll be astounded. I'll be so good that I'll be astounded....*

The white wolf lifted his head and howled.

The sound echoed in the lonely woods like a cry from her own heart. She swallowed on a shattered breath. Tears welled, unwanted nuisance tears, blurring her vision when she desperately needed to see.

The wolves circled closer. The word *run* screamed through her mind, but it was easier to think than act. She could hardly run hell-bent-for-leather wearing cross-country skis. There were trees all over the place, hardwoods as well as heavily branched pines, but her skis made climbing any of them just as impossible. There had to be a way out of this. She just had to *think.*

"Stand still. Don't run. Don't move—just stand real still."

She heard the human voice. A masculine voice, but just then she wasn't picky. One chord of that low masculine baritone and relief sang through her pulse like an opera aria. She whirled around. Nothing—not death, bombs or taxes—could have stopped her from aiming for that voice. "Oh, God, I'm so glad you're here—"

"For cripe's sakes, listen to me! *Don't move!*"

Two

Mary Ellen obediently froze. Her heart even started beating again. She recognized the giant from the restaurant, although she barely looked at him. Her eyes glued straight on the gun he was carrying. The nice, long, *big* gun. She wasn't going to die. The wolves weren't going to get her. He had a *gun*. "Shoot 'em, for pete's sake!"

"Now, just take it easy. I'm pretty sure we don't need to go that far."

His slow, lazy baritone took her back. "In case you haven't noticed—" personally, she thought he'd have to be myopic and deaf not to notice "—I think those wolves are planning to have me for lunch."

"Yeah, I can see they're not too happy with you." He glanced at the wolves, then back at her. "Try to see it from their viewpoint. A human is their worst enemy. And you didn't just barge into their territory.

You wandered within twenty-five yards from a nest of their pups. They're just trying to protect their young."

Conceivably he thought she needed this information. She waved her hand in front of his face. One of them seemed to be under the illusion they had time for a casual chitchat. It wasn't her. "I'm sorry I upset them. You'd never believe how sorry. If I could disappear into thin air, trust me, I'd be glad to. But that not being an option, I'd sure appreciate it if you'd at least *aim* that gun—"

"I'm afraid it isn't the kind of weapon you think it is. It's just a tranquilizing gun. No bullets. And yeah, I can shoot them if I have to, but it's a lousy choice. The sedative would put them out for several hours. They'd be prey to the elements, other animals, and they'd be affected by the drug for a couple of days. Just relax, okay? They aren't doing anything but growling at you. They're entitled to give you a lecture. You screwed up."

"Nothing new about that. It's the story of my life," she muttered.

"Pardon?"

"Nothing. I can't think. Geezle beezle, they're still circling!"

"I know. And I know you're scared, but you're staying real cool. I'm proud of you. Most men would have lost it by now, but not you. You're holding it together just fine. We're gonna keep talking, okay? And while we're talking, I want you to toe the catch on your skis. Real slow, real careful, see if you can get them off. Just forget the wolves. Look at me, straight at me."

He had everything wrong. She wasn't staying cool; she was a pinch away from totally losing it, and positively she'd done nothing to make the stranger—or anyone else—proud of her. Yet she looked straight at him, because he'd asked her. And she managed to awkwardly, clumsily toe off her skis, because he'd asked her to do that, too. The man had a Pied Piper voice—throaty and husky and hypnotizingly seductive. He could probably coax a nun to strip with that wickedly sexy voice, but that hardly explained why she obeyed him. There was only one possible reason why she did what he asked.

She'd lost her mind.

Circumstantial evidence wasn't a fair way to judge a man, but she could hardly fail to notice clues that he wasn't necessarily operating with a full deck. The wolves were snarling and circling and charging around. He was as calm as a spring breeze. Mary Ellen took that as a teensy hint that he needed a reality check. For reasons she couldn't imagine, the front of his parka and jeans were hard-packed with snow. The hood was thrown back, revealing a shaggy, disheveled pelt of jet black hair. It looked as if his hair was decorated with dry leaves, which made no sense. Making even less sense, he was unzipping his parka as he slowly walked toward her.

She'd instinctively trusted him in the restaurant, instinctively sensed that he wasn't the kind of man to prey on a vulnerable woman. Then and now, she should have remembered that her judgment about men wasn't worth a Las Vegas dollar. Obviously she'd been mistaken about the intelligence in his shrewd blue eyes. No way he could be too bright when it seemed to have missed his notice entirely that her life was in imminent danger. Hells bells, so was his. The wolves sounded restless and hungry and mean and ferocious.

And her damn fool of a giant was peeling off his jacket in freezing-lung temperatures as if he had nothing better to do.

"What I want you to do," he said gently, "is put on my coat."

"You want me to wear your coat?"

"And my muffler and gloves."

"And your muffler and gloves," she echoed. Vaguely she wondered if she'd landed in the twilight zone. She had experience, extensive experience, in embarrassing messes. Coping with situations that no sane woman would normally land herself in was really her forte. Somehow, though, nothing had prepared her for holding a witless conversation with a madman while surrounded by wolves.

"They know my scent."

"Swell."

Her deadpan comment was hardly intended to arouse his sense of humor, yet his mouth curved in the crack of a grin. "I'm getting the definite feeling we'd better backtrack a few yards. My name is Steve. Steve Rawlings. And I guess I just assumed you knew who I was. My being around has raised a lot of talk in town."

"I'm new in Eagle Falls. And not exactly on the chitchat gossip circuit."

He nodded. "So you didn't know.... These wolves are my problem. My job. By profession I'm an ethologist. I study and work with animals like wolves, and specifically I'm working with this pack. It'd be my responsibility if anyone was hurt because of them, and I'm for sure not going to let anything happen to you, okay?" He gave her a moment to take in that information, then calmly went on. "The reason I want you to wear my coat is that it has my scent. They know me. In fact I've known White Wolf, the alpha male, since he was a pup. I don't want to kid you—we're in dicey waters. Wolves aren't dogs—they're wild animals. It's dangerous to trust any wild animal. But I think we've got a great chance of this working.''

He'd reached her by then. The blasted man was so tall that she had to tilt her face to meet his eyes. ''If you're trying to be reassuring, I hate to tell you, but you're failing big time. I'm real close to throwing up.''

''Nah. You're staying real cool, real calm. I knew you would. When I saw you in the restaurant, I thought to myself, now there's a lady who wouldn't lose it in a crisis—no, no, quit looking at them. Look at me. Take it easy. You're doing just fine. Although—''

''Although?'' Momentarily she couldn't help feeling distracted. She wasn't the stay-cool type. She reliably fell apart in any crisis. Now was no different—she was scared enough to lose her cookies. How he could have formed such a mistakenly inaccurate impression of her was downright confounding.

''Although—'' lazy, easy humor glinted in his eyes again ''—it'd sure help a lot if you could loosen that death grip you've got on your ski poles.''

She glanced down. She had no idea her fists were glued to her ski poles until he started peeling her gloved hands loose. Once that was accomplished, the ski poles dropped in the snow. Then, with the gun anchored between his knees, he slowly fitted her arms into his parka. The size of his jacket was big enough to fit over her own, but stuffing her into the second coat was a cumbersome process. She couldn't help him. Her stomach was too busy doing flip-flops.

Her response to his closeness wasn't sexual. It couldn't be. Sex was the last thing on her mind, not just because of the situation, but just because. Other women seemed to feel an automatic jet pull near a virile male hunk. Not her. Her hormones had never flipped on like a light switch. She had to know a guy. She had to think about it.

Since sexual awareness couldn't conceivably be causing the dancing flutter in her stomach, she decided it must be the...strangeness. He'd given her a lot to take in. He worked with wolves. That was tough to imagine. He promised he wasn't going to let anything happen to her. It was even tougher to imagine her believing that—heaven knew, she'd suffered consequences from mistakenly trusting men's promises before.

She'd been reasonably fine. Until he moved so close. When he wrapped the scarf around her neck, his wrist brushed her cheek. The muffler carried the warm male scent of his skin, and his touch aroused a shivery lick of feminine nerves. She tried to prop Johnny's mental picture in her mind's eye, which invariably reminded her of the mistakes she'd made. Only it didn't work this time. Steve wasn't Johnny. He wasn't like any man she'd known before, and she had the sudden disoriented feeling that he could be far more dangerous than his wolves.

His towering height blocked the view of the woods, the world, the pale afternoon sun. She hadn't seen his face this close before. The weathered lines around his eyes and forehead were as ingrained as granite. He hadn't gotten those character lines playing checkers in a warm parlor. He knew what he wanted. It wasn't a life playing checkers. There was steel in his square jaw, wildness in his unkempt hair and rough, straggly brows. His touch was gentle with her, but she couldn't stop thinking that it didn't have to be. With his powerful build, she couldn't imagine anyone stopping him from doing whatever he wanted.

When he zipped the jacket straight to her chin, his eyes met hers. He didn't say, *Make up your mind, Mary Ellen.* He didn't say, *Damn, but I'm tempted to give you something a lot more serious to worry about than a few old wolves.* It was just in her mind, that he was sizing her up in an intense, intimate way. He didn't want her. For pete's sake, he didn't even know her. She was just imagining silly things because she was so shook up.

"They quit," she said.

"Quit?"

"The wolves. They're quiet. They quit howling." When he stepped back and glanced around, the breath whooshed out of her lungs. "I don't see them. Do you think they've left?"

"No. They're around. But since they've moved out of sight, they've apparently made up their minds to behave. Which leaves me with a tricky decision," he murmured.

Again, his eyes peeled on her. Again, she felt a curling sensation, as if her whole body was warmer than buttered toast. Foolishness. She was wrapped in double layers of down; naturally she was hot. It had nothing to do with the way he was looking at her. "What's this tricky decision?"

"I'm not about to leave you alone," he immediately reassured her. "I have a pickup over the next rise, about a quarter-mile walk from here. I'll take you home. But it would help a lot if you wouldn't mind sticking with me for a few more minutes."

"Sticking with you?"

"I'm in a bind," he admitted. "When I first heard the wolves kicking up a fuss, I was halfway through feeding the pups. There's seven of them, a couple I left hungry. It would take time to drive you home and get back here. It'd just be a lot easier to finish the job right now, but I don't know how shook-up or scared you are—"

She could have told him how scared and rattled she was. The instant she got home, she fully anticipated indulging in a nice long case of the shakes. She loved cats. She loved schnauzers. But this singular experience with wolves had permanently cured her of any desire to be anywhere near this particular animal again in this lifetime.

But damn. *He'd* saved her behind. Twice now. And he'd mentioned the pups, but she hadn't made the connection that he had anything to do with them. The debt she owed him sat on her conscience like guilt-laden lead, and geesh, what was a few more minutes of heart-hammering terror? "It's not that I'm shook-up," she assured him, and then had to clear her throat. The giant lie had almost caught in it. "But you're the one who needs to get out of the weather. You have to be freezing without your jacket. You'll catch cold."

Over his jeans, he was only wearing a gray alpaca sweater. The garment stretched over his muscular chest, a thick-weaved, scratchy wool, practical and warm enough for a dash outside but hardly for working in these temperatures. "I'm cold," he admitted, "but the pups are real young. So young that their survival at all is real iffy."

"So it could matter, if they were fed right this instant, huh?" She gulped in another guilty breath. Babies were babies. How could she be responsible for babies going hungry? Still, she'd only asked him a question. She hadn't said yes, sure, I'd love to stick around and risk my life for another few hours. Yet his response to her single hesitant comment was a devil-slow masculine grin.

"I could have guessed you'd say yes. Nothing much throws you, does it? And it's possible that we're pushing our luck, but I don't think so. White Wolf wouldn't have backed off if he hadn't made his mind up about you. Still, we'll just take this slow and easy. Have you ever seen baby wolves?"

No, she'd never seen baby wolves—or ever planned to. For two exhilarating seconds, her fragile ego basked in his respect for her courage, but that soaring sensation didn't last long. He was so totally mistaken. She hadn't earned that respect. She had no guts. She'd just never managed the assertive art of saying no—a personality flaw that had majorly contributed to her landing in hot water in the past.

She'd never been in hot water quite like this, though. Quicker than a smile, he'd taken her hand. Before she could draw a nervous breath, they were crossing the white sugarcoated valley. In the open. Easy prey for wolves or bears or anything else. He'd scooped both her skis and his gun under one arm, so it wasn't as if he could aim that rifle quick, even if he had to.

They climbed a ridge, ducked around a stand of white pines and scrambled down a knoll. The new snow layer was fluff, but beneath that lay an ice crust, tricky footing in just her ski boots. Even though he had to be freezing in just that sweater, he never moved fast and he never loosened his grip on her hand. The thick gloves prevented any personal contact, but his secure hold felt like being plugged into a direct socket of strength. He wasn't going to let her fall.

He kept talking in that lazy, calm baritone of his. Talking was a necessity, he told her. Wolves had acute hearing. Talking let the animals know where he was, who he was, and a steady, soothing tone helped communicate that he meant them no harm. Wolves were nervous by nature. They had reason to be.

Mary Ellen had no idea if he was successfully calming the beasts, but his low, husky voice was working an unwilling magic on her. He didn't talk about anything but the wolves. She wondered if he realized how much he was revealing about himself.

Isle Royale, he told her, was less than a thirty-mile stretch across Lake Superior from here. Since the late fifties, the island was one of the few places on the continent where the endangered species of gray wolf was protected. A few years ago, though, the species had started dying out. Numbers dropped from fifty to eleven. No one could pin down the problem. The wolves had an ample food supply; the winters weren't that harsh; neither disease nor age seemed to be the contributing factor. They simply weren't breeding. The best theory seemed to be genes—that the three surviving packs were too inbred. The wolves needed a new gene pool if they were going to survive.

"So two years ago, I flew in White Wolf. He's from Alaska—where I was working then. Carried him, his best girl and two more from that pack, and settled them on the island. They seemed to be doing fine.

They mated and bred, and everything was going hunky-dory—until this winter.''

Normally the icy waters of Lake Superior created a formidable barrier between the island and the Upper Peninsula. But that stretch of lake had frozen before, in winters as violently cold as this one. "The damn doofuses walked across on the ice floes. They got it in their heads that they wanted to set up housekeeping on this side. Not a brain in their idiot heads."

It was hard for Mary Ellen to think of wolves in affectionate terms like ''doofuses,'' but clearly Steve did.

"No one wants them. No one's ever wanted wolves. People don't mind a romantic story about them, like Jack London wrote or Walt Disney filmed, but find one in your backyard and that attitude changes real quickly. Man has always been afraid of wolves—it's as simple as that, and no laws have ever protected them from being hunted down. They *need* to be taken back to the island, partly because the whole species isn't going to make it—not without this new blood—and partly because their chance of surviving here is worse than a bookie's odds. So that's what I came here to do—transport them back to the island. Only damn, I hit a little snag I never expected."

"A snag?" She couldn't imagine what he'd consider "a little snag." He mentioned rounding up the wolves and transporting them to the island as if this were an ordinary project for him. Even trying to picture the act boggled her mind.

"White Wolf's mate was shot several days ago. And unfortunately, she'd just given birth to a litter of pups less than ten days before that."

"Someone shot the mother?" Her voice was small. Minutes before, *she'd* been in a bloodthirsty rush for him to aim that gun and shoot to kill. That white behemoth of a wolf—and his cronies—had terrified her. Still did. But she hadn't thought of the wolves as vulnerable then. She hadn't pictured a young mother hunted down, leaving a nest of helpless newborn babies. "I guess I should have expected that something had happened to the mother. I mean, obviously you wouldn't have any reason to be feeding the pups if the mom was alive."

"Well, normally if a mother wolf dies, another female in the pack will take over. She'll bond with the pups and start producing milk. Only there's only one other female in the pack. She's no spring chicken and that didn't happen. So I'm feeding them formula five times a day. Unfortunately they're just too young and weak to move right now. And the rest of the pack— they won't leave. Not without their young. There isn't a human alive who can understand a wolf's loyalty. He'll sacrifice his life to protect those he loves. They take care of each other. That instinct is as strong in wolves as their need to eat or breathe."

Steve grabbed her arm when she stumbled on a slick ridge. She hadn't been looking where she was going, but at him. His face was ruddy from the cold, yet the temperature didn't seem to bother him. He released her arm quickly, but the gesture had protected her from a fall as automatically as the wolves he'd been talking about. His affinity for the animals was no accident, she mused. He was like them. A lone wolf. A man who valued loyalty, who willingly made personal sacrifices for something he cared about, who was instinctively protective of others around him. He'd obviously chosen his work and his life-style. That kind of strength—that kind of loneliness—was beyond anything she knew.

But being a loner... Mary Ellen knew a lot about that. She'd lived her whole life with the tag of misfit.

"So," she said, "how long are you stuck with this problem?"

"It'll be at least a month, maybe more, before the pups are strong enough to be relocated. And the whole thing is a gamble. Someone would say a stupid gamble, trying to keep them together. It's not like I couldn't ship the pups off to some zoo—there's no problem finding people willing to take care of them. But they'd never make it outside of captivity if I separated them from the pack now. They imprint on the grown-ups. The older ones teach them how to survive in the wild, something no human could do. It's real iffy whether I can keep them all safe for that long. There's a town meeting this Thursday. I know damn well they have in mind voting an open season on my pals."

She glanced at him again. His voice never fluctuated from that slow, lazy drawl. He made that town meeting sound like nothing more challenging than a Sunday stroll. Yet it had to be hard, being an unwanted stranger with an unwanted cause, and she couldn't imagine the guts it would take to face down a townful of people who viewed him as an enemy.

She knew how it felt to be judged, so it was probably natural that she felt a compelling emotional tug for him. She was a loner, too, but a misfit not by choice. For an instant she wanted to reach out and touch him as if they shared a personal bond—when there was no bond. He had guts. She didn't. He had strength to burn, volunteered for difficult situations. Her response to the difficult situation with Johnny had been to cringe, get an itchy case of hives and then duck and run lickety-split, like the coward she was. She looked away. "I guess you've had to deal with that kind of problem before?"

He never got around to answering her, although when he suddenly stopped walking, she wasn't sure why. The craggy ridge looked no different than the landscape they'd just traveled—wild and woody. There were no footprints in the snow, no sign any human had ever discovered these primitive backwoods. The forest was dark, deep, endless, winding around hills and snow-swept, jutting crags of land. Then, though, she spotted an olive green box, like the kind of case people packed drinks and sandwiches for a picnic in.

Steve bent over and pushed the top off. The box definitely wasn't being used for picnic supplies. Strange-looking baby bottles were packed around hot-water sacks. He unwrapped one and showed her. "I got the bottles from the hospital in Houghton. They're meant for babies with cleft palates, but they work just as well for pups too young to suckle."

She edged closer, her arms wrapped around her chest. A wisp of a smell hit her nostrils—strong enough to make her nose crinkle.

He chuckled. "I should have warned you. The formula isn't exactly aromatic."

"Good grief, what's in it?"

"Piles of disgusting stuff, from raw egg yolks to vitamins. Trying to fool them that this is their mama's milk has been an uphill trip, I'll tell you. But never mind that. Are you ready to fall in love?"

Her eyes flew to his faster than a shooting comet. "I beg your pardon?"

Slowly, lazily, he studied her face as if the color in her cheeks was the most fascinating thing he'd seen in a blue moon. "You're not all that sure what you think, are you? You don't think you're gonna be tempted into caring. A lot of people don't. A wolf's a wolf, and these little guys don't come out of the womb looking like a Walt Disney cartoon. They're born wild and wary, a real handful, no interest in being tamed. But I just have this strange feeling, Mary Ellen, that you're gonna fall hopelessly in love."

He was talking about the baby wolves, of course. Not him. Not them. Not for a moment—not even for a millisecond—had she thought he meant anything else. It was just the low timbre in his voice when he said her name . . . she didn't realize he even knew her name . . . that made her suddenly shiver. She shifted her attention from his gaze at the speed of light, looking all over for some sign of the nest or a den or someplace where the pups might be. "So where are they?" she asked impatiently.

"Right here." Stuffing two bottles under his sweater, he bent under the shadowed branches of a spruce, and then went belly flat in the snow.

More wary than curious, she crouched down, too.

"Can't see them from that far. You have to get closer."

Well, geesh. She'd come this far, so it seemed pretty ridiculous to back out now. Snow showered her head when she elbow crawled to his side, protected by ski pants and a double layer of coats, as he certainly wasn't. She heard him sneeze, and automatically started to respond with a "Bless you" when she saw the silky gleam of tiny eyes.

The nest wasn't exactly a cave, more like a long, low ledge of a rock that tunneled in several yards, the opening concealed entirely by the spruce and stark winter black brush. Once inside, the darkness was as sudden as night. Her pupils had to dilate to see anything after the blinding glare of sunlit snow. Yet she saw the tiny eyes, and then another pair and another. Milky blue. Baby blue. The fur balls were nestled in a heap, with tiny shiny noses and tiny floppy ears, and one had the same gorgeous white pelt of his father.

The snowball baby tried out a lonely, angry howl, echoing his daddy except that its volume was barely a mewl. He thought he was real tough, for a two-pound bit of fluff. Steve plugged its mouth with the strange-tipped bottle, and the baby instantly quieted. Steve sneezed again—the blasted man was positively going to catch pneumonia on this little venture—but sympathy for him wasn't the reason for the velvet lump in her throat.

Damnation if he wasn't right.

She fell hopelessly in love on the spot. Not for him. Good grief! She wasn't crazy.

But definitely for the babies.

Three

Predictably, as soon as Mary Ellen doused the car lights, she dropped the keys. Bending over and squished, she groped in the no-man's land of the dark car floor until she found them, then collected her gloves, shoulder bag, hot pads and Crockpot. Holding all of those, she naturally discovered she had no way to open the door. She rejuggled. Eventually she escaped the dratted car, and holding the heavy pot with both hands, gave the door a good swing with her fanny to close it.

It was a lot of trouble to go through, just to bring a man some plain old beef stew. Well, truthfully it was her best ragout, but that point was moot. The dinner was owed. She hadn't met any Galahads in the nineties. Steve had not only given up his coat for her yesterday, but he'd also saved her from the wolves—both in the woods and the bar. She obviously had to find a way to thank him.

The offer to bring him dinner had been impulsive. Steve had pounced on it. No demurring. No gee-you-don't-have-to's. His fast agreement worried her—it was the first time she'd seen Steve Rawlings do anything fast—and she'd chewed a fingernail, fussing over whether he could misinterpret the gesture. Men had a habit of misinterpreting just about anything she'd ever done, no matter how innocent or well-intentioned.

Her arms ached from the weight of the Crockpot as she looked around. He was home, because she could see the edge of his black four-wheel-drive pickup, parked behind the trailer. Yellow light shined from the windows, making lonely patches of color in the snow. Even this early in the evening—six o'clock—the night was blacker than tar. He'd chosen to set the trailer in the middle of nowhere, isolated in a nest of black trees and sooty shadows. An icy, eerie wind shivered through the treetops, making her shiver uneasily, too.

If she were home in Georgia, it'd be warm by the first week in March. Not blizzard-mean-cold like here. In her Georgia hometown, too, no single woman would be visiting a single guy, in his lair, after dark, unless she was volunteering for big-time trouble.

Now that's ridiculous, Mary Ellen told herself impatiently. She wasn't staying. She was just going to drop off the Crockpot. Twice now, he'd gone out of his way to help her, and manners required a thank-you. The only danger she was risking was a frostbit tush from standing out here in the dark like a witless goose.

She took a breath, marched to his doorstep and used her elbow to knock. The knock only created a muffled sound, but the door promptly flew open. Warm air flooded out. She only had one quick, daunting glimpse of a giant whose shoulders were never meant to fit in a compact trailer-size door.

"Finally Red Riding Hood arrives. I was starting to get worried, afraid you'd get lost trying to find the place."

"Red...?" The Riding Hood tag startled her. Could he possibly know how wary she felt about walking into a wolf's lair? But then she caught the flash of an easy, teasing grin, and it clicked real quick where he'd picked up the fairy-tale association. She *was* wearing a hooded cherry red jacket and carrying goodies through the woods. Pretty hard to deny she was natural prey for a tease, and she had to smile back. "No, I had no trouble. Your directions were great."

He reached down the steps to take the heavy pot from her hands. "This smells great. Come on in."

She shook her head swiftly. "I can't stay—"

"You have to work tonight?"

"No. I only work four nights a week. It's just that I only meant to bring you dinner. To thank you. Not to take up any of your time—"

"You're going to make me eat alone? When you're already here? And I haven't had anyone to talk to all day but wild animals?"

His mournful tone made her roll her eyes—he couldn't pass that off as blarney in Ireland—but damn. He made her feel awkward about taking off without at least sharing some conversation. Gingerly she stepped inside. "I'll just stay a couple of minutes," she insisted.

He didn't seem to hear her, and he hadn't let go of the pot yet. He sniffed. "I haven't had a homemade ragout in a hundred years. Is it okay if I admit my undying love for you?''

"It's just stew," she said dryly, but drat the man, he was downright forcing her to chuckle.

"Just stew is real food. You don't understand. I've either been opening cans or eating Samson's cooking for weeks now.'' Once he set the pot down, he hustled her out of her red jacket and made it disappear, then gave her white tunic sweater and jeans a once-over. She'd been careful about her choice of clothes. The jeans were old, not tight, not fancy, and the bulky sweater concealed her figure more effectively than a nun's habit. There was nothing in his view, absolutely nothing, to cause the sudden lazy, masculine gleam in his eyes. "Good thing you're a shrimp. There's not a lot of space around here for two of us to move around.''

She chuckled again, and this time felt the tension in her shoulders easing. Would a man call a woman a shrimp if he had seduction on his mind? He was being funny, natural, just plain nice. It was past time she kiboshed the electric nerves she felt around him. She never used to be so paranoid, not until Johnny burned her, and it was ridiculously egotistical to imagine that Steve represented any danger to her. He was positively nothing like Johnny.

"Your place isn't so small. In fact, it's a lot bigger than it looks on the outside," she commented as she looked around.

"So sit and make yourself comfortable. You can have the seat of honor. You want wine, beer, soda?''

"Nothing, really, but thanks." His "seat of honor" was the only chair, a tweedy recliner in gray hues. A long couch matched it. Both were his size—heck, she could have curled up and slept in the chair—and the small living area overlooked the kitchen ell. The bar-style table was ivory colored, the charcoal-shaded carpeting cushion-thick. A short hallway of closets led to a shadowed bedroom—where he'd tossed her jacket—and she saw the tucked end of a Hudson Bay blanket in the wedge of light.

The trailer wasn't big enough for a party, but there was ample room for him to move around. It *was* hard for two to maneuver, though. She slipped off her boots and dropped in the chair when she saw she was going to be in his way. He opened and closed cupboards, taking out plates, silverware, napkins. His TV was on, tuned to the news, but without sound. He kept up an easy conversation.

"I have a place in Wyoming. A little house, on a spread of land by a creek. That's where I grew up, out West, but I've had the trailer for years. Sometimes I'm gone months at a time with my work, and I'd go nuts trying to live in motels and finding rental places. This way I can have my own stuff with me."

"So... you go wherever the wolves are?"

"Not always wolves. But they're my love, and I seemed to have ended up specializing in them whether I planned it or not. I worked for the EPA for a while, then hooked up with the National Park Service. For this project I've been loaned out to the state of Michigan—their DNR, Department of Natural Resources. Never seems to matter who's signing my paychecks, I end up doing the same thing. There just aren't a lot of people who get real excited about tackling a wounded wolf, or moving a pack of 'em. Maybe it's like a doc who overspecialized. There's nobody else who does the job—or really wants the job—so I'm the stuckee."

"You've traveled all over?"

"From Mexico to Alaska," he confirmed. "The red wolf, gray wolf, Mexican wolf—they're all threatened. Only three places on the planet where they're not, though lots of people are sympathetic to the cause. The UP here has really worked at it—set up a Michigan Wolf Recovery Team, and backed that up with good laws and stiff penalties for killing wolves. But the bottom line is that when a wolf's causing trouble, the easiest solution is to shoot him—or trap and put him in captivity, out of harm's way. Nobody's to blame for that. A problem wolf, wild, part of his pack, in his own environment...he doesn't make it real easy to help him. It's just a lot easier for someone who knows the species to take the ball."

"So Wolf Man gets called?" she murmured.

"So you heard what they've been calling me in town." He ladled out two plates of stew and set them on the counter. "Actually I've been called a hell of a lot worse. Come on over. You're going to share this with me, aren't you?"

Actually she wasn't hungry, and for sure she'd never planned on sharing dinner. Yet she leveled a plate of ragout along with him, and an hour passed before she even noticed they were still talking, mostly about his work. Surely other people were fascinated by his wolves? Yet every time she asked another question, she found the strangest smile on his face. A slow smile. A slow, sneaky, irresistibly masculine smile. As if she were passing some test she didn't even know she was taking.

Maybe she was testing him a little, too, becoming more intrigued by this stranger she was coming to know. His work sounded exotic and dangerous and lonely. But it suited him. His quiet confidence was a measure of strength, not arrogance. He'd found his niche in life, was secure in what he wanted, who he was as a man.

She liked him. Honestly, simply, liked him. Even those slow, sexy smiles weren't enough to make her nervous around him again—or to stop her from being nosy. Pure feminine curiosity had her gaze prowling around the place, noticing things she'd missed at first.

The trailer was definitely a man's den, but it wasn't impersonal. Photographs were crammed on top of the TV. One of a man and a woman, both older, wearing Western-style clothes—his parents? And another photo showed a pair of teenage girls, arms hooked around each other's shoulders, hamming it up with sassy smiles for the camera. She saw his rifle, cradled in a rack over the door. And a mess of books, heaped on the carpet by his chair. The whole place carried the starkly masculine scents of leather and wool, which struck her as a humorous contrast to the look of the baby bottles drying in his sink. An antiquated blender took up space on his counter; stealing more space was a long sack of a yellow, floury-looking substance. She suspected it must be the base for his formula.

"I can't believe I forgot to ask... how're my babies doing?"

He chuckled. "*Your* babies—the little rat finks— clawed my hand pretty good this afternoon. I can only hold two bottles at a time. One of the little she-wolves got impatient about waiting her turn."

"It had to be a she-wolf, didn't it? I swear, women always get blamed for everything."

"Hey. You're taking *her* side, when I'm the one who got wounded?"

"I saw the two itsy-bitsy scratches, Rawlings. I'd say it's a real stretch to call that wounded." Teasing him, being natural around him, was coming easier. Truthfully she'd noticed the small red scratches, the same way she'd noticed his strong capable hands, his butter-soft chamois shirt, his black-lashed incredible blue eyes, the way his old jeans hugged his flat behind when he moved. But she was trying not to notice those things, trying hard not to be aware of him in the wrong way. "Do you still have to feed the pups tonight?"

"Yeah. Once more." He rinsed the plates, a two-second job, and then carried over a pot of coffee and two mugs. "In a few more days, I hope to hell I can cut out this last night feeding. It's a real pain in the keester."

She frowned. "You're really stuck with these pups, aren't you? I mean, they're dependent on you. And there's no one to take over if you get sick."

"The solution to that is easy. I just won't get sick. I've got a tougher problem than that. It takes a blender to mix up the blasted formula, and that old monster's been quitting on me twice a day," he said dryly.

"The blender?" She glanced at the appliance on the counter. "I could take a look at it, if you want."

"Beg your pardon?"

"I fix things. Electronic stuff is what I love, but I'm not too bad with small motors and things like that."

He just looked at her.

"Really," she said. "In fact, that's what I've been trying to do since I moved here—start a fix-it and repair business. I only took the job at Samson's because it was the only work I could find. It'll take some time before I can build up the kind of business I want.''

She suddenly wrapped her hands tightly around the coffee mug, wishing she'd shut up. Out of sheer stubbornness when she moved here, she'd hung a shingle outside the house—so her budding repair business was no secret—but letting her dream out of hiding had predictable results so far. Just like at home, fixing things wasn't supposed to be a feminine occupation. Men, especially, seemed to feel her mechanical interests required a joke or a cute comment. For sure, they doubted her skill and had a hard time taking her seriously.

She was braced for the same reaction from Steve. And didn't get it. He looked at her another second, and then faster than she could blink, swung around, grabbed the blender and plopped it in front of her. "You don't know how much I appreciate this. The thing's been driving me nuts. Give me a wolf, give me a bear, give me an avalanche, I do just fine. Get me anywhere near something mechanical and I fail big time."

"Steve, I really can't guarantee—"

"Whatcha need? Tools? I have a drawerful. Haven't a clue what they're for, mind you, but there has to be something you could use.... So, you moved here to start a business? Where are you from?"

"White Sands, Georgia. A very small town. South of Savannah, near the coast." It didn't take five minutes for her to have parts strewn all over his clean ivory counter. Like a surgeon's nurse, he kept feeding her tools, rags, oil and respectful awe. She was pretty sure the awe was faked—to keep her working—but it kept her smiling anyway. "I thought a fix-it lady might have a chance around here. Small town, not a lot of stores, and the economy isn't exactly booming. People are more inclined to repair things that break down instead of automatically buying new."

"Hmm. It had to take a lot of guts. Pulling up stakes like that, moving somewhere this far from your home."

She didn't glance up. It wasn't the first time he'd formed a completely mistaken conception of her. She'd moved because she was a yellow-bellied coward, not because of any admirable adventurous spirit. She considered being honest with him. But to admit she'd been jilted and had a long history of disappointing everyone around her?

Not in *this* lifetime. She plopped down the screwdriver. "Okay. Plug it in and let's give it a try."

He plugged in the blender and tried the switch. The thing roared like nobody's business. "Hot damn—and don't waste your time telling me how you did that. I don't want to know. I don't care . . . just, how are you on leaky faucets?"

"Rawlings, for pete's sake, *anyone* can fix a leaky faucet."

"I guess it's too much to ask, huh? Never mind—"

He didn't have a leaky faucet. He had a leaky pipe. Like most fix-it problems, the repair didn't require a man's brawn but simply a few practical brains and ingenuity. She just didn't exactly anticipate laying on her back under the sink in his small bathroom, working with a crescent wrench, pail and gunk, surrounded by all the personal masculine things that had to be uprooted from his small cabinet, ranging from condoms—how embarrassing!—to shaving lotion and aspirin and TP and ace bandages and first-aid supplies. Steve was a big help.

He held the flashlight.

She gave him a quick primer course on plumbing, thinking she was helping him out. Just the basics. Knocking and rattling usually meant a loose washer; a whistle sound meant a stem threading was going bad; a left-hand thread was the clue when you were looking for the hot-water faucet. She quit trying, after catching a look at his face. His mind was so quick, his eyes so full of shrewd, sharp intelligence. Not about this.

"Nothing's getting through, is it?" she asked dryly.

"Hey, I'm listening. Dialectic unions, close nipples, male and female parts—"

She rolled her eyes. "Just hold the flashlight, Rawlings."

"Yes, ma'am."

Finally she was done, and squeezed out of the contortionist's nook with her hair flying every which way.

"I don't know how to thank you."

"No problem. What are friends for?" A swipe with the rag, and the cabinet floor was dry again. She had to wash her hands, and he had some things to put away, but both fix-it missions had been successful. Her heart filled with buoyant exhilaration. She'd owed him, and managed to find a real way to be of help and pay him back.

When she spun around from the sink, though, she discovered that Steve hadn't moved. He was still on his haunches, the flashlight still dangling from his hand, and his eyes were on her face. He'd looked at her that way before. She'd been mercilessly careful not to misinterpret that look before, too.

"You're something special, you know that?" he asked quietly.

Her pulse suddenly thrummed and her cheeks flushed. It wasn't the first time she'd discovered that it was tempting, irresistibly tempting, to bask in his warm praise. But she knew the truth. She wasn't special. He was the one doing something extraordinary with his life, a man who was impossibly easy to respect. She was glad, fiercely glad, that they were still relative strangers and he didn't really know her, and she moved swiftly toward the door. "Gee, I didn't realize how late it was. I'd better be going, and you still have to get formula ready for the last feeding tonight, right?"

"Right."

She hustled into her jacket and gloves almost as fast as Steve had hustled her out of them hours before. When he grabbed his coat, she insisted she didn't need to be walked out to her car. He had things to do. No problem. He could return the pot whenever he got around to it, or just bring it to the bar if he was regularly in Samson's.

Ignoring her, he yanked on his coat and walked her outside. The woods were steeped in velvet darkness, cedar and pine scents fragrant in the night air, the sky winking a thousand stars. She was far too busy to notice.

They'd been doing just fine, Steve thought, until he'd dared give her a compliment. Then she'd flown—and was still flying. He watched her fumbling in her shoulder bag for her car keys, making more nervous chatter than a magpie. How to reheat the stew. What to do if the blender malfunctioned on him again.

"Mary?"

She could barely find time to glance at him, she was so busy trying to find that car key. "It's Mary Ellen, actually. The other day I meant to ask you how you knew my name, but you must have picked it up from my name tag at the bar, right? Listen—thanks for everything. For what you did for me in the bar the other night. For what you did in the woods. I want you to know—"

"Mary," he repeated again, and this time something in his voice finally snagged her attention. Still, she obviously wasn't expecting him to gently hook a knuckle under her chin. Her face tilted. Her eyes shone with sudden naked vulnerability, winsomely soft and unsure.

Steve hadn't been sure, until that moment, that he was going to kiss her. Once he did, he was damned aggravated with himself for waiting so long.

If she'd been kissed before—and she must have been, must have done a lot more than kissing at her age—it didn't show. Her mouth was warm, the bottom lip a cushioned pad for his to sink into. He tasted coffee and sugar. Mostly sugar. That flavor was no surprise, not when he'd seen nothing in her nature so far but an unbearably sweet sensitivity to everything and everyone around her. She didn't move away; she didn't argue about his right to take that kiss. Instead she went still, holding-her-breath still, as if she just had no idea what to do with an alien pair of lips invading her private space.

He did. Her jacket hood fell back, revealing a glossy tumble of mink brown hair for the moonlight, for him. His fingers slid into her hair as his mouth brushed gently on hers, wooing gentle, infinitely nonthreatening, a kiss that said don't be scared, it's just me.

He understood her wariness; hell, his whole life was spent handling wary, wild creatures. They had no reason to want a man's hand on them. Man had power; man was the dominant enemy and their most dangerous predator. Mary Ellen shivered when the pad of his thumb caressed her soft white throat. Maybe she instinctively understood that she was in that kind of primitive danger, because he wanted a hell of a lot more than a few tame kisses.

Her fingers fisted on his jacket, hanging on tight when his tongue traced the length of her bottom lip, sipped of her flavor and texture and then sneaked, real slow, inside.

Tentatively, shyly, her tongue met his. Just as hesitantly, her hands loosened that clutch hold on his jacket, climbed up his shoulders and wrapped around his neck. A whisper-sweet kiss turned damp and intimate. And suddenly he had gold.

She didn't seem to expect it.

He did. The moonlight glowed silver on her pale face as she arched against him, as if buffeted by a sudden, wild, lonely wind. No one else was anywhere around. There was just her and him, and in that darkness, a fire of tension that built with stunning speed. Her mouth turned fluid under his, wet and warm. He took a kiss that involved tongues and teeth. She tugged his head down for another.

Her responsiveness made his blood rush hot and fast. He knew what passion was. He'd been drawn to women before, but not like this. This was like sliding down a snow hill with the power of an avalanche, a toboggan run straight to another dimension. Her hair tumbled through his fingers, as silky as the texture of her mouth. His hands swept down, hampered by her bulky wool coat, yet he could feel the heat radiating from her body, the electric awareness. Stars fell around them, louder than thudding thunder. At least that was the only way he could account for the sudden roaring in his ears.

He had a sixth sense for trouble. And he'd hoped she was going to be this kind of trouble, hoped there was fire under that soft mouth, but damned if he'd let himself dream he'd find gold like this. At some point he'd known he was going to test it. He had to know if he was imagining the connection, dreaming it because he was lonesome and hungry for a woman, or if what he guessed about her was right.

Now he knew. He lifted his head, finally, reluctantly. He was rock hard. So rock-painful hard that he had to smile. The air was colder than an ice bath; both of them were packed in layers of winter gear, and still she'd made him hotter than a volatile blaze and from only a few kisses.

He hadn't been mistaken about her.

Her eyes had a dazed cloudiness. Her lips were still parted, wet, damp and dark from the pressure of his. She looked...confused, as if what had just happened couldn't possibly have, as if she expected to click her heels three times and end up safely back in Kansas. Possibly she'd wasted a lot of time kissing desk jockeys and insurance salesman. Possibly, just possibly, she might be coming to some unexpected conclusions about why those nice, tame guys had never satisfied her.

He bussed her nose. "You're the most special woman I've met in a long time."

"I—"

He waited, but all she did was swallow. Her eyes darted to his, then shied away. Her moonlit face was flushed. "You have your car keys?" he asked her.

Yeah, she had her car keys. She seemed astonished to find them still clutched in her hand.

"You know where you are? Know how to get home?"

She nodded. He shoveled his hands into his pockets as he watched her climb into the car, back up and finally disappear from sight.

He had formula to make, baby wolves to feed, a long night ahead of him. Still, he stood there, letting his body slowly cool down. The taste of her clung to his memory. He wanted to savor the feel of her, the look of her, as long as he could.

He'd surprised her with that kiss. That was dirty pool, stealing an embrace from a woman before she had time to erect defenses, time to say no. Still, there was neither guilt nor regret on his conscience.

She was a mouse. That was the outward image she projected, what he'd first thought her, too—a shy, scared mouse with no self-confidence or backbone in sight. For damn sure that was how she saw herself. Someone or something must have wounded the lady and wounded her deep, but apparently it had been a real long time since she'd looked in a mirror.

If she didn't see the strength, the specialness, the uniqueness of Mary Ellen Barnett, he sure as hell did. No mouse took off from her home to live alone in the back of beyond. She'd taken a job that scared her. She'd been scared in the woods, too, by White Wolf and his pack, but damned if she hadn't shown more stand-up guts than ten men. He saw the truth about her, all right, but the poor baby didn't realize the really fatal mistake she'd made.

So carefully, so deliberately, he'd told her about his work tonight. He'd expected her to turn tail and run. Other women always had. Finding a woman to share his bed had never been a problem, and that had been enough in his twenties. But he was thirty-three now, old enough to value—to crave—something lasting, deep, real. He'd about given up believing that he'd ever find a woman who wasn't intimidated by the danger and isolation of his life-style. He never blamed any of them. Hell, if he were a woman, he'd have run from a guy like him, too.

But Mary Ellen hadn't run. She'd listened. Listened and accepted automatically what he did, accepted *him* like no woman had in his memory. Maybe she didn't understand what she'd given him. It was dangerous to offer a lone wolf kindness, and showing him how much wild abandon lay beneath that shy first layer... he was afraid, seriously afraid, that that was a mistake he wasn't going to let her take back.

Who knew how far they could go together? She had secrets, he sensed, some kind of trouble in her past that had badly wounded her self-confidence. Winning her trust could be an uphill battle. Still, everything that ever mattered to him, he'd had to buck the tide and fight for. No battle had ever scared him yet.

If he'd learned anything from being a misfit and a loner, it was that when a man found buried treasure, he'd be damned stupid to let it go.

Four

———

Going anywhere near him again was a mistake.

Mary Ellen tossed a roll of antacids into her purse—she'd been popping a lot of antacids in the past two days—and then grabbed her coat. It wasn't as if she *had* to go anywhere. Normally on Thursdays her shift at the bar began at four, but Samson was temporarily closing down for the town meeting. Afterward, the bar was guaranteed to be packed. If she had a brain in her head, she'd be sitting in her rocker, feet up, relaxing and resting for what was guaranteed to be a long work night. Positively it was a witless, stupid, insane move to go anywhere near Steve Rawlings again.

She buttoned her jacket, then opened her purse to unwrap another antacid. It was not a good sign that her stomach was churning before she'd even left home. An even worse sign, that she was still headed toward the door.

She'd talked herself into worrying that Steve would be all alone at that town meeting. Was that stupid or what? As if he'd have no one in his corner if she didn't go. As if her being there could possibly matter a fig. She had no possible way to offer him practical support—she didn't know diddly squat about his business or his wolves or his problems—and he had no reason to expect her there.

She was known for making stupid mistakes in judgment, but this one really took the cake. Maybe she couldn't shake the troublesome, nagging mental picture of him facing the whole town alone. But that was blurring the only issue that mattered. An intelligent woman—a woman with an ounce of common sense—steered clear of a man she was afraid of.

Mr. Rawlings scared her silly.

No man had ever kissed her that way. And no man had better try it again—including him, *especially* him—or else.

Scowling, she popped the second antacid and then stalled in the doorway, glancing around, hoping she'd discover some chore that needed doing and would keep her home. There was nothing. The blasted place was all in order—at least, as she defined "order."

The four-room cabin had been used as a rental hunting lodge for years. Samson owned it. The last time Samson had dropped by with his wife, his hound-dog jaw had dropped five feet and he'd howled a disgusted, "Honey, what have you done?"

She'd cleaned a dozen years of kitchen grime and dust; that's what she'd done. She'd put up lemon yellow curtains in the windows and a rug on the kitchen floor, taken down the dreadful horns over the huge stone fireplace, added a woman-size rocker and hung

Monet prints all over the rough log walls. It had taken three days scrubbing to get the tarnish off the old brass bed, but now it shined and was covered in a fluffy white comforter with eyelet lace. The watered blues and greens in the fireplace rug added color and softness.

Samson claimed she'd ruined a perfectly good man's hideout. She sure hoped so. Nothing matched; she didn't care. For the first time in her life, she wasn't trying to please anyone else—although one corner of the living room definitely looked like a rummage sale.

Tools and parts lay scattered. Several people in town actually had responded to her ads and signs, and her repair business was starting to take off. As she'd expected, though, the start-up process had some pitfalls. Mrs. LaBelle had brought her ailing vacuum; Harold Becker had shown up with a misbehaving VCR. Both were legitimate customers, but Richard Schneider had carried in a perfectly functioning ham radio, and used the visit as an excuse to chase her around the kitchen. And one of Fred Claire's cronies—Mr. Squirrel-faced Stelmach—had been under the mistaken impression that she'd put together his mail-order stereo system for free if he provided a bottle of wine and made a pass at her.

You're dithering, Mary Ellen. You already know you're rotten at handling men. Johnny proved that long before you came here. Which is all the more reason to fish or cut bait—are you really going to be a damn fool and go to this meeting or be a good, intelligent, sensible woman and stay home?

Apparently she had no sense. Jaw locked, a frown embedded in her forehead, she locked the cabin door and headed for her car. Her mood was darker than a well pit, and the drive into town was no help. Snow fell, sticking to the windshield wipers and making visibility tricky. The roads were slushy and slick.

He'd be alone against the crowd. Her heart just couldn't seem to ignore that. She'd always been a misfit, always alone in a crowd herself.

But maybe he kissed every woman that way. He was a sexy, virile man. He was adorable. He'd probably kissed millions of women and just chose that particular gesture to thank her for dinner. It wasn't necessarily his fault that embrace had made her personal stars move. He didn't necessarily *know* how startlingly, frighteningly, powerfully she'd felt in his arms. He'd been kind before that. She'd felt safe with him. She was making too much of an embrace that he'd probably forgotten in the flash of a second.

It was like trying to talk herself through a crash landing—she was feeling much better about handling the whole situation—when she saw the parking lot. Her fingers groped blindly for another antacid. The meeting was being held in the old frame schoolhouse, and the lot was crammed full. Apparently the whole population of Eagle Falls was already inside. She parked her car on the street—there was no other spot—and hiked toward the building with her head ducked against the bitter wind.

Even before she opened the door, she heard voices raised in anger. No one glanced up when she slipped inside, trying to be quiet and unobtrusive as she pulled off her gloves and searched for a place to sit. The cafeteria benches were all pulled down, all packed, the room lit with harsh fluorescent lights and smelling of wet wool and hot emotions. She whispered "Excuse me" as she moved past bodies, finally finding a place to stand in the back between two burly men in hunting clothes.

Her heart was pounding. No way to settle it down. Steve hadn't noticed her—maybe he never would in this sardine-packed crowd—but as she'd been afraid, he was up there alone. And the group was as revved up and agitated as her own heartbeat.

Her eyes softened, looking at him. The two of them were like Mutt and Jeff, the idea of a relationship between them downright humorous—but that didn't mean she couldn't respect and admire him. Wearing a buffalo-checked flannel shirt and jeans, he was dressed no differently than the other men, but Lord, he was. Everyone was huffing and puffing but him. Her lone wolf was still, his eyes quiet, his voice calm and unbudgeably patient.

"...You don't want wolves in your backyard. I understand, but this is only a temporary situation until I can get the pack moved back to the island. I know you're afraid—but so are they. A wolf would never voluntarily choose to be near people. These guys never meant to land in your neighborhood—they were just stalled here when this litter of pups was born. Since I've been here, you haven't seen any of them near town, now have you? They have no reason to come any closer unless they're hungry, and that's not going to happen—I'm supplying them with all the fresh meat they can eat. Unless they *have* to hunt, they *want* to stick close to their young. They just have no reason at all to be anywhere near the town borders—"

A woman's shrill voice interrupted him. "I have two kids under the age of ten, Mr. Rawlings. I'm afraid to let them outside to play. You *say* they won't come around here, but you can't guarantee what they're going to do!''

Mary Ellen swallowed hard. If she'd been a mother, she'd have felt the exact same concern. Wanting to be on Steve's side didn't change her own uneasiness about the adult wolves, but good grief. The crowd had worked themselves up long before she walked in, and it was a frightening lynch-mob mood, no one listening.

A man's voice bellowed, ''I say we form a hunting party and shoot them!'' His bellow echoed in a rallying cry of ''Shoot them'' through the room. ''We don't want them near our kids and womenfolk! Nobody's safe as long as they're around! Not even our pets!'' And another, ''I say, kill 'em!''

The raised voices picked up momentum until Steve said quietly, ''You could do that.'' Frowns responded to his comment, then silence. It was obviously not what they were expecting him to say, and he went on. ''There are four adults. Seven pups. I'm not going to quote laws to you. You all know the species is protected. You also know that laws or not, you could probably wipe out the whole pack and nobody'd catch you. So you can make that choice. I sure can't stop you.''

Steve's gaze scanned the crowd, identifying faces, waiting until the last mutterings died down completely. Then he talked again. ''There's another choice. In a matter of days, I could pack off the pups to a zoo, trap the grown wolves and fly them to Isle Royale. Since that would solve the problem, I'd like you to know why I haven't made that choice.''

He paused. ''These pups—this one litter of pups— could affect the whole future of the wolves on the island. The wolves are in trouble right now, dying off, so inbred that they've quit reproducing. These pups represent a fresh bloodline, which could make all the difference—but not if I separate them from their family now. All I'm asking is your patience for a few short weeks. If I take the cubs away from their family, they'll never make it outside of captivity again, because they won't imprint or learn the behavior they need to survive. Is there another way to bring fresh bloodlines to the island? Sure. And those plans are in the mill, but they just can't happen fast enough. It takes time to find and set up another pack, time for them to breed and produce young, and that time is a critical factor when survival of the wolves on the island is already in jeopardy." He paused again. "Still, you're not personally affected by any of that, are you? I mean—why should you care?"

He saw her. Right when his gaze landed on her face, she was popping another antacid and was scrunched tight between the bear-size shoulders on both sides of her. The room, she suddenly realized, was unbearably hot and short on oxygen. His eyes met hers, touched hers, and wouldn't let go. She read his glance: *I knew you'd be here.* She saw a roguish grin come and go so quickly that no one else probably noticed it. And the devil looked at her in a way that rattled her feminine nerves and reminded her—so unfairly!—of an embrace she'd been working overtime to forget.

Yet he never took a breath, never stopped talking. "Alaska is one of the three places on our planet where wolves are supposed to be safe, yet an authorized wolf kill went on their legislative table last winter. For a fifteen-dollar license, hunters could use seaplanes, semiautomatic assault rifles, snowmobiles—anything they wanted—and no limit on the wolves they could kill. Where I come from, using a semiautomatic assault rifle isn't hunting. It's not sport—it's slaughter. The objective of this kill was to save a herd of caribou for hunters—an understandable goal, considering that hunters are a major boon to Alaska's economy. Except that there was no shortage of caribou—the species was thriving—in all the traditional hunting spots. Killing these wolves never made logical sense. And their survival as a species is a real precarious 'if'—even if man leaves them completely alone.''

He waited, then said quietly, ''You don't have to care. You don't have to make that your problem. And I get as impatient as you do with radical environmentalists who put animal concerns over people. People matter more—but there isn't an animal on the planet who isn't biologically linked to our own human survival. And unless somebody gives a damn, we're going to lose one of the most beautiful creatures on earth.''

With a stricken feeling of shock, Mary Ellen noticed the time on the wall clock. More than an hour had passed. The meeting could be over any second. She *had* to leave. Samson expected the crowd to flood in his direction, and she'd promised to open the bar.

She tried to catch Steve's eye, and couldn't. Not that it mattered. As she should have known, her coming at all had been silly. Thinking he needed her was a joke. Imagining that she could have somehow helped him was downright comedic. Her lone wolf had turned that crowd into lambs right in front of her eyes—it boggled the mind, considering she'd never been in a public situation where she hadn't ended up with egg on her face.

She desperately wanted to know how the meeting turned out, but there was no chance to find out.

Two hours later, her feet hurt, the decibel level in the bar was enough to make her ears ring and the cigar and cigarette smoke was eye-stinging thick, even back in the kitchen section. Wearing an apron over her ski sweater and jeans, she flipped another four patties on the grill. The meat sizzled and spit.

"Another three T-bones, sweetheart," Samson called back. "Two still kicking—blood rare—and the other joker wants his destroyed. Don't short the garlic."

"Sure," she said, although the grill was so packed she hadn't a clue where to put them. Sweat tickled the back of her neck and itched. The sock in her right boot had bunched and sure as petunias was going to cause her a blister. Anything, though, was better than working out front. None of the men bothered her back here—except for Samson, who kept lumbering past with his white hair flying like a halo, squeezing her shoulder or thumping her back affectionately. Mary Ellen suspected that Samson had never had a female employee before. He never seemed sure whether to treat her like one of the guys or like an honorary grandfather.

He was in grandfather mode tonight. With business booming, he was happy. Mrs. Samson was out front somewhere, yelling at him to *sit down* or he'd be crippled with arthritis in the morning. Samson ignored her, just winked and rolled his eyes every time he got the royal command.

The back door suddenly opened, letting in a gush of welcomed cold air. She didn't look up for a second, simply couldn't. She had an assembly line going of plates, buns, lettuce, pickles and burgers, with a clothespinned list of orders waving at her from eye level. She didn't really know anyone was there, until a hand shot out and stole a potato chip from one of the plates.

She swatted the hand instinctively, and earned a grin in response. *His* grin. His gaze only took two seconds to prowl her damp cheeks and chewed-off lipstick and tired eyes—she *had* to look frazzled, and nothing of her figure showed under the cook's apron. Yet the gleam in Steve's eyes registered male appreciation in capital letters. She wondered if he was myopic. She wondered why her toes were suddenly curling. She wondered what the Sam Hill he was doing in Samson's kitchen.

"I had to thank you. For coming to the meeting," he explained.

"I only wish you had something to thank me for. I didn't do anything." She shifted three plates to the open window under the heat lamp, where Samson would pick them up for the customers. When she turned back, Steve had installed himself in front of the grill and was reading her order list, still wearing his alpaca jacket.

"You need three steaks on?"

"T-bones. I'm getting them." She hustled toward the refrigerator. "You can't be back here. Samson'll have a stroke if he finds you in the kitchen."

"Samson'll never know. I did a stint as a short-order cook in college, so don't worry, I won't mess you up... and yeah, you helped by coming. I wasn't ex-

pecting to see any friendly faces in that crowd. Yours
mattered. And your showing up mattered to me. This
guy really wants double pickles, huh?"

"Sweet, not dill." It was like trying to budge a
mountain—or work around one—and arguing with
him had about the same effect. "I didn't say or do
anything to help you."

"You were there. In my corner." He shuffled lettuce on the buns as efficiently as he might deal a deck
of cards, but he glanced at her. As if he liked the idea
of her in his corner. As if he liked the idea of personally, privately cornering her even more.

Her cheeks flushed. "Hold the onions on that one."

"Okay."

"I had no choice about leaving the meeting
early—"

"I guessed it was a work night for you."

"They were all calmed down when I left. You have
a way of making people listen, Rawlings."

"Yup. A hotshot orator, that's me." He popped a
chip into her mouth with a playful grin. "You haven't
had a chance to eat yet, have you?"

She had to chew and swallow before answering.
"There'll be a lull sometime. I'll get a chance to eat
later." Her mind was still on the meeting. "Do you
think it'll be okay? That they'll leave the wolves
alone?"

"I haven't a clue. It could go either way. People, like
wolves, behave different in a pack than when you get
them alone. Groups bring out the worst in guys like
Fred Claire, who's always got to prove how macho he
is. Hunting my babies probably sounds like a real
macho sport to him—especially if he's egged on by his
cronies. But there are some terrific people here. Right

now there are more wolves in the UP than on the island, which says a lot about the local population—how tolerant and sympathetic they are. Or how sympathetic they *want* to be.''

Mary Ellen understood. ''They're afraid.''

''Yeah, and people never behave as rationally when they're afraid. It would help a whole lot if that doofus of a mother-wolf hadn't dropped her litter near the town border. Can't expect a mother with two kids under ten years old to *not* be nervous with a wolf pack in spitting distance from her back porch. I can reassure her until doomsday that the wolves have absolutely no interest in any confrontation with humans. But why should that mama trust me or believe anything I say? I'm a stranger.''

She hustled three more plates to the window, then whirled around to turn the T-bones—only to discover that Steve had already done it. She stole a studying glance at his face. Maybe he was talking about wolves and mamas, but she had the strangest intuition that he was trying to communicate something else—like that he understood *her* feelings, about thinking he was a stranger and she had no reason to trust him.

But she did. From the first, she'd felt an instant and instinctive trust for Steve. He was a man of integrity and strength and courage, a man who protected and would never prey on those weaker than him. And her original impression and judgment about him hadn't changed; it was just those kisses. Safety suddenly became a relative term. A woman who exposed herself to a hurricane wind was begging for trouble. Whether or not anyone *intended* for her to be hurt, it could happen.

She wasn't afraid that he was interested in her, but becoming badly, increasingly afraid that she could care for him—seriously, deeply care. And tarnation, with her history, she knew better than to let her heart gallop ahead of her common sense.

"You're not working out front tonight," he commented.

"No. Samson and I switch off on kitchen duties. He likes to be around the crowd, and they're buzzing tonight. All talking about your meeting, I suspect."

Apparently Steve had lost interest in talking any more about the town meeting. "The guys give you a lot of trouble?" he asked casually.

"You mean like the other night? Heavens, no. Fred Claire just had too much drink. It was nothing." She ducked her head, so he couldn't see that whopper of a lie plastered on her face.

"If you haven't worked in a bar before, I imagine it could be a little tough going."

"For sure it isn't my choice of career," she admitted, "but it's putting groceries on the table. And Samson and his wife have been wonderful to me."

"Then you're not having any trouble handling the wolves, hmm?"

"Are you kidding? Piece of cake. I'm twenty-seven—"

"Yeah?"

"Hardly a wet-behind-the-ears teenager. I can handle myself." She shook extra pepper on the next order of burgers, well aware she was heaping lies on top of lies. She even knew why. The confounding man had aroused her feminine pride. Heaven knew how Steve had gotten the insane impression that she was strong and gutsy. But he liked those qualities in her, respected her for them. And gloomily she heard herself shoveling it on even thicker. "None of the guys have really bothered me. A few jokes, that's all. Water off a duck's back."

"Yeah? Funny, I would have guessed they'd give you a real hard time. Not many single women around here. And none remotely as pretty as you are."

"Pretty?" She had to chuckle—that time, an honest chuckle. "More like plain old ordinary, and when I'm around here, I'm usually running around too fast for anyone to notice me anyway."

The steaks were done; he forked them onto plates and she added slit baked potatoes, then whisked them to the window. "Well, if you don't need any help handling *those* wolves, I was wondering if you might be interested in handling the real ones. Any chance you'd like to come with me tomorrow to feed the pups?"

She wasn't expecting the invitation, and it came right when she felt flustered—flustered because of all that lie telling, flustered because he'd called her pretty, and downright nervous because their hips and hands kept bumping in the minuscule working area in front of the grill. The cramped little kitchen was hot, but it hadn't been nine-hundred degrees. Not until he came in. She wiped her damp palms on her apron, thinking that she'd barely known her own name since he came in. That was the only excuse she could conjure up for saying, "Sure. What time?"

"Around one o'clock is their usual midday feeding. I could pick you up at your place."

"Okay," she said.

That one, small, innocent word was all she said. Nothing to earn that slow charge of a masculine grin.

And before she could protest, he bent down, brushed her temple with a whiskery kiss and grinned again. "I'll be damned. I've never had a woman give me a 'yes' to that particular offer. Not once. We're talking virgin territory. You're gonna have to promise to be gentle with me, because I'm suddenly feeling tongue-tied. I was *that* sure you were going to say no. I never even met a woman before who wasn't afraid of taking on my wolves."

He left minutes later. She touched her temple with two shaky fingers—still feeling the imprint of his lips, the sudden rush when his scent and texture and touch had seemed to surround her. She let out a loud, gusty sigh. Mr. Rawlings wasn't going to have a tongue-tied problem around women in this lifetime. His experience teasing the female half of the species was more than obvious. And this time, she positively wasn't going to overreact and imagine a mountain out of a simple, single, camaraderie-type kiss.

If her heart was racing and her knees were feeling shakier than limp noodles, there was a logical reason for it. His wolf cubs were irresistible. Something about those cubs made her maternal instincts go turbo—she was crazy about the little suckers. But an experienced coward, such as herself, had a predictable allergic reaction to anything dangerous. If she went with Steve to see the pups, she risked a confrontation with the adult wolves in that pack again.

That nervous reaction, she told herself, had nothing to do with seeing Steve again.

It was the wolves she was worried about.

Not him.

Five

It always struck Mary Ellen as the granddaddy of all ironies that she'd been born with a natural talent for fixing things, when she couldn't seem to fix herself. Flaws in her character resisted all attempts at change.

Undoubtedly that was why she found herself in the woods with Steve. Scared out of her mind, in a situation she could easily have avoided, smiling brilliantly while the palms inside her mittens were slick with nervous sweat. "Gee, I thought maybe the wolves wouldn't be around. I mean...they could have been busy hunting somewhere. Or taking a nice snoozy afternoon nap."

Steve chuckled. "They wouldn't likely be hunting—or napping—with us around. They can pick up smells, like a human scent, from more than a mile away. They've been tracking us ever since we left the truck, just didn't decide to show themselves until now. I'm guessing they'd like to meet you.''

She had to swallow twice to get past the barbed-wire lump in her throat. They were still yards from the pups' den, but close enough that she recognized the landscape—the white birch with the lightning scar, the stand of fat, thick spruces and firs, the snowy ridge with a marshmallow glaze on a sun-blinding winter afternoon. Just like before, too, there were shadows on the ridge above them.

White Wolf stood poised and alert and still, assuming the leader position ahead of the others, his luminous dark eyes focused straight on her from above. His sidekicks flanked him, but they weren't so quiet. Their fangs were bared; their growls coming low and menacing, and they were pawing the ground as if they planned to lunge down the ridge any second.

Mary Ellen swallowed again, but a high-speed plunger wasn't likely to budge that lump in her throat. ''You think they want to meet me, huh?''

''Yup. In fact, I brought some bones you could give them for a treat. Figured if you were going to be around them, it was about time you made friends.''

''Bones,'' Mary Ellen echoed, thinking of her own fragile ones and that it was time she exercised some honesty. Her ego had more holes than a sieve after that last humiliation with Johnny. Unquestionably Steve's good opinion worked like a salve on her wounded pride. She liked his believing she was strong and self-reliant. She liked his respect. It just seemed the ideal opportunity to mention that she was the most gutless female cookie to ever come down the pike.

''You're not afraid, are you?''

"Who, me?" She wanted to have that heavyweight truthful discussion with him. She really did. Temporarily, she was just so busy. Her gaze was glued on White Wolf as tightly as the binding on a book. And the wolf, she could have sworn, was staring right back.

She'd read somewhere that a wolf's eyes were hypnotizing, but his pals didn't give her that problem. It was just him. He was so damned *wondrous,* the dark eyes such a contrast to his ruffled white fur, so much sleek-muscled power cloaked in that luxurious coat. Her fascination with him kept building. He always distanced himself a few yards from the others, as if accustomed to the loneliness of being a leader. That loneliness touched her, and the intelligence and mesmerizing quality in his satin-soft eyes was almost— unnervingly—human. He met her gaze as if taking her measure.

She could have told him what her measure was. She was crazy about him—but that didn't stop the adrenaline from gushing through her pulse. She couldn't inhale. She couldn't exhale. Never mind how beautiful he was, never mind this strange empathetic draw she felt for him . . . if he chose to take one short leap from that ridge, she could easily picture herself as his afternoon snack. And that was a ditto for his cronies.

"The streaky dark gray one—she's Scarlett," Steve said casually. "The name seemed to fit her. She's sassy and spoiled, the darling of the pack. All the boys bring her food and treats. She's got them believing she's the prettiest girl in the county, which was a pretty easy sell considering she's temporarily the only adult female. And the light gray one with the crooked tail—he's Thunder."

"That's nice."

"Thunder is the low man on the totem pole, the last one to eat, the guy everybody takes out a bad mood on. Every pack has one especially submissive member—somebody's got to be at the bottom—but Thunder has the strength and size to rise in the pecking order. Just not the character. He makes a lot of noise, but he's just a wuss."

"That's nice."

"Then the one standing closest to White Wolf—the one with the blue eyes and the real white face—he's Hamlet. Everything has to be a drama with him. He has to argue and think out everything, just can't do anything the easy way. Mary?"

"What?"

"You're doing just fine," Steve said gently. "There's a trick with dealing with predators. You probably know it better than I do, since you're a woman and you've had to handle those guys in the bar. If you show fear, it makes you prey. One-on-one, a wolf isn't usually unfriendly—he's curious, he's smart and by nature he's a sociable creature. But in a pack, now, you get different behavior. They act more aggressive in a group. They can smell fear, and when they smell fear coming from another animal, it triggers their aggressiveness."

"We definitely wouldn't want to do that," Mary Ellen managed weakly.

Steve smiled reassuringly at her—as he slowly unpried her fingers from his coat sleeve. "And you're with me, so I know you're not afraid. You know I wouldn't let anything happen to you." As if that completely settled the issue, he hefted a canvas sack into her arms. "Moose bones. Their favorite. And believe me, they know what you have—they can smell the bones from here. Just toss them out, okay?"

She heard out that plan. She had a much better idea. "The pups are probably hungry. How about if *you* do this bone thing, while I just quietly hustle over to the sled and start getting the bottles together—"

"Nah. We want the wolves to see these bones are coming from you. It'll help them identify you as a friend."

"Ah." The rank, ripe stink emanating from the canvas bag lacked any claim to aromatic, but in went her hand. If she couldn't get out of this—and blast and damn, she *really* didn't want Steve to know what a coward she was—a new survival theory was called for. She'd just throw the bones five miles or so. Far. Real far.

As hard as she hurled the first bone, it landed about eight feet away—a short eight feet—not even to the top of the ridge. She assumed White Wolf, being the boss, would claim first dibs on the loot, but the big guy never moved from that sentinel post where he was watching her. The dark gray wolf named Scarlett sprang for it, leaping on the bone in a snarling frenzy.

The back of Mary Ellen's neck drizzled dampness. Her hands moved in a blur, trying to get rid of those bones quickly, hurling them faster than a Las Vegas dealer could deal out a hand of blackjack.

To her horror, Steve deserted her. Which she didn't realize until she dared risk a millisecond glance, and discovered the heartless wretch had backed away a full foot behind her—a full foot!—and was talking quietly and calmly the whole time.

"Attagirl. I know all that growling and snarling sounds intimidating, but you have to remember that they can't talk. They have to depend on sounds and certain behavior to do all their communicating. Packs are big on dominance. White Wolf—he's the alpha male, the top gun. The others will obey anything he says, so you'd think he'd be the meanest guy in the pack, wouldn't you? That's what people used to think who studied wolves, that the alpha male won his status by fighting his way to the top—but it's more complicated than that. The truth is that the rest of the pack love him.''

''Love?'' Slowly she was starting to breathe easier. God knew what was going to happen when she ran out of bone treats, but, temporarily, for sure, the wolves had completely lost interest in her. Still, it was a major mental reach to associate the concept of ''love'' with any of their behavior.

''Yeah, love,'' Steve repeated. ''If they didn't love him, they wouldn't follow him. Strength isn't enough to get elected king of the pack. He has to prove to the others that he'll take care of them, that they can trust him to lead—but they would never obey a dictator. I'm not saying they aren't a little afraid of him, but fear of the dominant male is natural in any species. No alpha male has ever won his title by being a tyrant. They have to love him— Are you running out of bones?''

''Yes. That's the last one.''

''Good. Sweetie, you did great.'' He not only strode back to her side, but acted as if she'd accomplished something monumental—like solving the hunger problem in Africa. He squeezed her shoulders in an enthusiastic hug.

There was no kiss, just that companionable hug. But it was happening again, she thought dismally.

Anywhere near him, she forgot about all the sensible, logical things she should be afraid of. Instead, as if it were a critical factor in her life, she noticed the snow-flakes drifting into his hair. She noticed the dance and darkness in his eyes, the wicked allure in his slow, seductive grin. And geesh, when he looked at her a certain way, she felt a wild pounding in her pulse, a drumbeat of both fear and anticipation, and a flush-hot sensation down to her toes.

Talk about insanity. He wasn't for her, and it wasn't as if she had any illusions on that score. The right woman for Steve needed to be his equal—a risk taker, a woman strong in character and self-assurance—not someone who was just pretending to have those qualities. Maybe she'd fooled him, but she hadn't fooled herself. Still, her feelings for him kept building, unasked for, unwanted, as sneaky as a kitten's purr.

His relationship with that big monster of a wolf, she thought, was part of the problem. Every time he talked about White Wolf she was struck by the similarities. Both were alpha males. Both had pride and strength and that invisible something that separated them from the others in their species. Loneliness and loyalty were an integral part of their natures. And when he mentioned fear of the dominant male, she'd intuitively understood what he meant. She'd always had a strange, disquieting electric feeling around him, an instinct that arousing a wolf's passions could be dangerous, that making love with Steve would be real, real different than anything she'd known with Johnny or any other man.

Was her imagination running amok or what? Steve had given her absolutely no reason to fear him. There'd only been that one embrace, and since then,

he'd proven to be an extraordinarily gentle man—
gentle with her, gentle with everyone and everything
around him, and incredibly natural to be with. Like
now.

"Well," he said dryly, "are you ready to take on the
little hellions?"

"Hey. Watch what names you call my babies,
buster." Relieved to have the excuse, she broke away
from that dangerously compelling hug and jogged
over to the dish-shaped sled that Steve had pulled behind his skis. A little distance between them was all it
took to restore her equilibrium. Food was strapped to
the sled—both food for the adult wolves and the in-
sulated container holding the cubs' dinner. She lifted
out a bottle and started shaking it. "Do you think
there's any chance my angels are awake?"

"Trust me. They're not angels. And we're not quite
ready to go in there yet. The first thing we need to do
is transform you into Mae West."

"I beg your pardon?"

He grinned. "You're willing to carry some of the
bottles, aren't you? Generally I unzip my jacket and
stuff 'em next to my chest. That way, the milk keeps
warm a little longer, and both your hands are still free
to move around." He paused. "If you want some
help—"

There was no heavyweight look in his eyes now, just
sheer masculine mischief. *That* kind of teasing, she
could handle blindfolded. "Thank you, but I can stuff
my own bra. I practised enough when I was thirteen."

"Did you?"

She flipped him a hand gesture, unzipped her jacket
and started padding in bottles. The result was a lumpy,
misshapen bosom that made her chuckle. "Well, it's

the size I was praying for when I was a teenager, but not quite the shape.'' She glanced at Steve, who was stuffing his jacket the same way, and chuckled again. "I hate to tell you this, Rawlings, but you couldn't pass for a woman if your life depended on it.''

"Hey. Are you laughing at me?'' he demanded.

She was. There now, she thought, it wasn't that hard to think of him as a friend, to *be* a friend. Steve was alone. So was she. If she locked her mind on that road and ignored the temptation to be sidetracked down other directions, everything should be fine.

Temporarily that was easy. Crawling on her belly to get to the pups' den was the same clumsy process as the first time. Ducking overhead branches and brush, she was huffing and puffing by the time she reached the pitch-darkness under the ledge overhang.

Steve paused when she did, lying elbow-touching distance from her side. Both of them waited until their pupils dilated. The smell in the cavelike hollow was earthy and wild, not an unpleasant odor but only strange. Once seconds passed, Mary Ellen could make out the nestled heap of pups . . . and then one lifted its head.

She recognized White Wolf's son—or daughter— from the white scruffy fur and eyes softer than satin, awake, alert and staring right at her. The pup climbed to his feet, no steadier than a drunken sailor, weaving and shaky legged. He promptly fell on his behind but got right back up again and tried out a warning growl for his human visitors. The howl had the same volume as a kitten's mew, and his fluff ball of a tail was wagging so hard that he knocked himself down.

"Oh, God," she whispered, "I fell for him the first time. But I don't think I've ever been as hopelessly in love as this."

Steve had rolled on his back and was already unzipping his jacket to pull out the first bottle, but his eyes were on her face, not the pup, not any of the pups. "I feel," he said, "exactly the same way."

They both charged through her door as soon as she unlocked it, shedding boots and parkas and winter gear at the same time. They were both tired, cold and starved. For three days now, Mary Ellen had come with him to feed the pups in the afternoon, but Steve was dominantly aware that this was the first time she'd let him inside her place.

She hustled ahead of him, switching on a lamp, kicking a shoe out of sight under the couch and trying to finger some order into her disheveled hair at the same time. "Make yourself at home. I warned you not to expect anything fancy, didn't I? Sunday nights, I never fuss much. All I made was a pot of chili—"

So she'd warned him. Several times. "I'm hungry enough to chew on raw leather. Chili couldn't possibly sound better."

She grinned. "Well, I'm pretty sure I can promise you it'll be better than raw leather—and it'll just take a few minutes to throw a salad together. I'm trying to think what I have around here to drink—soda or coffee or wine? Does a glass of red wine sound okay? I'm still so freezing that I'd like something to take the chill off."

"Wine sounds fine. Do you want me to help you with the salad or start a fire?"

"The fire, for sure, if you wouldn't mind. There's a box of long matches right by the kindling—"

"I'll find it." He hunkered down by the hearth and started layering cedar chips and kindling, but not before taking a long look around. He saw her work corner—all kinds of electronic parts and mysterious tools stashed on a table. He also saw the Monet prints on the log walls, the ankle-deep plush rug in pastel blues and greens, the fragile vase of dried bluebells. The contrast between her practical, mechanical side and her love of pastels no longer surprised him. And he could have guessed that she'd somehow make a home, even out of an old, cold, dark hunting lodge.

One of these days, though, Steve had to figure out why such a totally feminine woman was hiding out in a log cabin in the middle of nowhere. Soon. In fact, preferably—hopefully—tonight.

He struck a match. The fire took with a *whoosh*, filling the room with the fragrant smells of cedar and pine. He settled back, watching her. She was flying around the kitchen at racing speeds, but not so fast he couldn't check out the fit of her jeans. The denim fabric was old, soft, sexy, snuggling zealously over her long legs and pert fanny. The cowl-necked red sweater matched the color in her cheeks, and the angora texture cupped her breasts as faithfully as he'd like to. Mary shot questions at him—enough to keep a conversation going without his having to think about it.

"The bottle says Pinot Noir. Samson gave it to me, said the bottle was just gathering dust in the bar—that crowd never orders anything but whiskey and beer—but I haven't a clue what it is. You know anything about wines?"

"I'm no expert, but I'm pretty sure it's a dry red."

"It'll go with chili okay?"

"Sure."

"What do you think—a honey-mustard dressing or ranch?"

"Whatever you have around is fine by me."

"I can set plates at the table here. Or if you're still cold, we could just as easily eat on the coffee table by the fire—"

"By the fire sounds great." He hadn't kissed her since that first time, hadn't tried. Fear had made him behave. Her fear, not his. He was still struggling to understand why she was so scared of him.

She was natural and easy with him now, but that was only, Steve suspected, because he'd found the confounded trick to make her relax. His whole nature was to protect and shield the vulnerable. A man automatically protected a woman. Those were masculine rules he lived by, an attitude and nature he took for granted. Until her.

It went against his entire grain to throw Mary Ellen to the wolves...but that insane technique worked. Although it made no logical sense, her confidence and comfort level with him had only started happening when he threw his white-knight rules out the door.

Most women were intimidated by being associated with a leper, but she'd shown up at that town meeting and given him her support. In the bar he'd seen firsthand that she was skittish around men, yet when he'd sneaked that first kiss—a totally unprincipled and aggressive pass—she responded with the explosive firepower of TNT. And when he deserted her alone with the wolves, knowing damn well she was scared, she'd stuck out that adorable chin and thrived on the challenge.

Following that line of reasoning, Steve considered that he just might be able to coax her to fall in love with him—if he threw her off a cliff.

Unlike the sane, logical, rational women he'd known in the past, Mary Ellen not only warmed up, but damn near *glowed* with sassy confidence when she was forced to do things she was afraid of. Maybe conquering challenges was important to her? Maybe handling fear was some kind of private test? Who knew? All Steve really understood was that his soft-eyed lady had the guts to tackle anything. With one tiny exception.

Him. Mary Ellen got real wary, real nervous—hell, the lady hid behind a brick wall—when she sensed he was interested in being more than pals with her.

Undoubtedly she'd only let him inside the house tonight because she was finally convinced he wasn't going to give her any trouble. Poor baby. She really didn't look prepared to be thrown off a cliff. As she carried the wooden tray to the coffee table and set it down, her cheeks were flushed and her smile was as innocent as sunshine.

"Whew. Thank heavens it's warm here by the fire. I'm a long way from Georgia," she said with a laugh. "Until I moved here, I'd only seen snow a few times."

"I'll bet you miss your family." He poured the wine while she settled on her knees, ladling chili into deep-dish bowls.

"I do miss them, but I talk to my mom and dad a couple times a week on the phone. I'm adopted, did I tell you that?"

"No." But he was strongly conscious that she hadn't volunteered any personal information about herself before.

"My biological parents died in a car crash. I was adopted when I was about two. Mom and Dad grew up in the sixties, took me on with all kinds of wonderful idealistic theories about being sensitive, understanding parents. Poor darlings." She dived into the chili. "I think they envisioned long, deep talks over the kitchen table. Only I never seemed to be the kind of daughter where those kinds of talks did any good. I was always a problem. Fought with the boys, wanted to build tree houses instead of dollhouses, always came home covered in mud. And then there was the time I accidentally set my bedroom on fire..."

"Yeah?" He had to grin.

"I was just trying to rewire it. I was eleven at the time, fascinated by electricity and fixing things... They came home from work to the fire trucks and police." She sighed, then carted out more stories in the same humorous Southern drawl.

He heard about the school play, where she was a rabbit in the front line who fell off the stage. He heard about the day she got her driver's license and plowed the car straight into the garage wall. She was trying to make him laugh, Steve suspected, and he did.

By the time they'd devoured the salad and chili, though, he couldn't fail to notice that all the stories had a common theme. They were things she'd done wrong. Embarrassing things. Shared with droll, dry humor, but it was almost as if she were determined he knew that she was a cutup and misfit and no kind of woman he could possibly be romantically interested in.

"Anyway..." She pushed her empty dish aside and stretched her stockinged toes toward the fire. "My parents are wonderful people. And I adore them. But I could never seem to do anything they expected or were prepared for. I'm afraid they were stuck with a real changeling."

"I know what that feels like." When he saw her glass was empty, he poured her more wine. "I get on with my dad about as well as a bear and a cougar in the same territory. The ranch has been in the family for three generations. I have two younger sisters, but I'm the only son. My dad had big expectations that I'd carry on the tradition, only, to save my life I couldn't conjure up any interest in the ranching business. When I was a teenager, I could be in the same room with my dad for all of five minutes before we were in a fight."

"All of five minutes, huh?"

"He's a good man. I respect him and love him to hell. But we've never been able to communicate, not sure we ever will. I grew up feeling like a misfit."

"That's exactly how I felt." For the first time since dinner started, she met his eyes. He heard the same love and loyalty for her family that he felt for his own—and the same feeling of isolation and separation. The empathetic connection always seemed to surprise her.

Not him. On the surface they were as different as a fragile rose and a blundering bull, but from the beginning he'd sensed the kindred understanding between them.

The firelight made her skin look ivory, her eyes the silky blue of a lake at midnight. She knew, he thought. She *had* to know there was enough sexual voltage in the room to power a nuclear reactor. And he'd been as good as a Boy Scout, understanding that she needed time to get to know him, but they'd moved miles past being strangers now. Surely they could move past go? She was special. Rare. He'd been alone too long *not* to realize how special and rare she was. And all he wanted was to let her know how he felt.

Maybe she sensed that nasty cliff coming. Because her gaze suddenly skittered away and she bounced to her feet faster than a gazelle in flight. "Dishes," she said.

"Dishes?" He glanced down at the tray of dinner debris and thought *damn.*

"It's okay, you don't have to help."

And be in dutch with her for the rest of his life? He carried the loaded tray to the kitchen and installed himself in front of the sink. He washed. She dried and put away. Outside, the night sky had darkened to coal, and it was snowing, fat crystally flakes that stuck to the windows and driveled down to a mound on her sill. Inside, there was an island of light. At least, Steve thought, where she was.

Waiting for him to finish the last pot, she peered outside, standing on tiptoe. "I can't *believe* it's snowing again. The roads are going to be icy. Do you still have to feed the pups again tonight?"

"Yeah, one last time, but not for a few hours yet." He glanced at her. "It really doesn't scare you, does it? Living out here alone, in such an isolated spot?"

She shook her head. "No way. I love the woods, the country, and as far as being alone, I can take care of myself. And it's the first time I've really been on my own. I like it all—the independence, the privacy." She motioned to her fix-it corner and chuckled. "And the freedom to make messes that couldn't possibly bother anybody else."

"No one special that you miss from home?" he asked casually. He handed her the dripping pot, which she immediately started rubbing with a towel.

"Well, sure. My family and friends—"

"I meant a man."

"Oh. Well . . . there was." She crouched down to fit the pot in a bottom cupboard. "I was engaged, but that's definitely over now. And for right now, freedom suits me just fine."

So, there'd been a man. A recent man. Steve dried his hands on the towel and switched off the kitchen light. The window reflected silvery shadows on her expressive face. He sensed the ex-fiancé was a critical clue to understanding his mystery lady, but every instinct warned him not to push her further. At least not about that guy.

"Freedom always suited me, too. Although studying my wolves has given me a whole perspective on freedom that I never had before." He grinned. "I won't stay much longer. But how about if I fix your fire and we have one more short glass of wine? I have to tell you about my wolves and how they dance."

"Dance?"

"Yeah," he said, "dance."

Six

"Come on. Wolves don't *really* dance."

"Yeah, they do." Steve fed the fire a couple of choice oak logs, and then stretched out beside her on the thick rug. Shadows flickered on the far walls, on the stone hearth, on her face. She'd not only brought two fresh glasses of wine, he noticed, but about the instant he announced that he was leaving soon, she'd completely relaxed. Soon, of course, was a relative term. At the moment, he wouldn't have stirred from her side for a bomb.

"This dance is something they do when they're choosing a mate," he told her. "I've only seen the ritual once. It was in Alaska. The alpha male is the only guy in the pack who gets to mate, did I tell you that before? And this alpha male was a big gray I called Romeo, had a real proud and dignified type of personality. Usually. He turned into a total bungling doofus when he fell for this dove-colored young honey."

When Mary Ellen chuckled at that image, he reached behind her head to turn off the couch lamp. "You don't mind, do you? The light was really glaring in my eyes."

"No, it was glaring in my eyes, too. Get back to the romance, Rawlings," she said impatiently.

"Well ... Juliet knew that Romeo was interested. Personally I think a she-wolf makes up her mind at first sight as far as what she feels, what she's gonna let him do. But it wouldn't be cool for her to let on. Maybe he's the dominant male, maybe she's even a little afraid of him, but she's the boss as far as love goes. And they both know that."

The coals glowed in the hush of fire. When he stretched back on his elbows, she did, too, her eyes sleepy and her skin iridescent in the soft firelight. He suspected the long hours outside that afternoon were finally catching up with her, because she'd never been this completely at ease with him before. Whether she realized it, he was trying to tell her a lot more than just a story about wolves.

"Juliet let the big gray track her for miles, ignoring him the whole time. When he finally collapsed for a nap, though, she chose that moment to walk past him and flick her tail right in his nose—picture a man poleaxed after downing a fifth of scotch, because that's how powerfully her scent gets to him. And that's the beginning, the first sign he's had that she might, just might, be willing to let him court her. After that, Romeo would kiss her and pet her and parade in front of her, showing off his stuff, looking cool, being macho...and she'd tease him right back. Neither of them were eating or hunting or paying attention to any of their pals in the pack, as if this game they had with each other was the only thing that mattered on earth."

Steve took a sip of wine, then put his glass—and hers—on the coffee table. "When Juliet was ready, though, when she *finally* made up her mind...she did this dance for him. Frisking around, leaping in the air, just acting exhilarated and full of sassy hell. And when she was done—Romeo had been watching her the whole time—he got up and did one for her."

"It was really? Like a dance?" Mary Ellen asked.

"Not a ballroom waltz, but yeah. There was a rhythm and grace and pattern to what they were doing. And their eyes—their eyes were only on each other. That dance, of course, was only the beginning of the real love affair. One of the things I've found fascinating about wolves is that they make love differently than any other animal in the kingdom."

"You're kidding. How so?"

"Most animals only take a few minutes to mate. Biologically speaking, there's an excellent reason for that fast speed. They're vulnerable to the elements and prey when they're hooked up together. Nature essentially protects them by making the process speedy. And wolves could do it that way. They just don't. They make love slow, real slow. Maybe the female knows that she's risking being hurt to dance with a wolf. Maybe he realizes that she's scared. But for whatever reason, he makes damn sure her pleasure is prolonged with that slow pace."

Mary Ellen frowned. "You thought all this, just from watching those two wolves?"

Hell, no, he'd thought up most of those details from watching *her*. The story about the wolves and their dance was certainly true. It was just that wolves, right then, were the last thing on his mind. Mary was lying a breath's distance away from him. She'd invited him in, offered him dinner and wine, had no objection when he'd switched off all the lights. But every instinct told Steve that she had no idea he was going to kiss her. He was happy she felt safe with him, happy she'd finally come to trust him, but completely confounded how she kept missing even the most blatant clues he sent out. He was interested. Intimately, carnally, emotionally, and in every other way interested. In her.

When he lifted a strand of hair from her cheek, she smiled.

When he tilted his head, she was still smiling.

When he angled his mouth, only an inch away from her soft, warm lips, her eyes shot wide with surprise. It finally seemed to occur to her that she was in trouble.

Big trouble.

His fingers slid along her jaw, into her hair. Slowly his mouth touched down and connected with that nectar-sweet softness. He'd picked her from the pack. That's what his first kiss told her. The second kiss was as slow as a shiver, a whispery caress, a promise that he wasn't going to rush her, that she could set any old pace she wanted, even tease him from here to hell if that was what she was in the mood for, and he wouldn't push.

But the invitation was there.

For her to dance with him.

"Steve," she whispered on the catch of a breath.

He should have known. Put her anywhere near the dangerous edge of a cliff, and she dived straight off.

When Mary Ellen forgot those insecurities haunting her and dropped her guard, she wasn't afraid of anything. Arousing the wild animal in a man came as naturally to her as breathing.

Her fingertips touched his whiskered cheeks, then sieved into his hair, pulling him closer. She was asking for a deeper, darker kiss, and being a gentleman, he obliged her. If she'd asked him for the moon, right then, he'd have found some way to give her that, too. He'd half believed that first embrace had been a fantasy and a fluke, his response to her colored by loneliness and frustrated hormones. He was wrong. It had been no fluke, no fantasy.

She was real. And she tasted so good that it was the avalanche all over again. That same rumbling roar filled his ears as he bore her down, flat into the cushioned rug, her responsiveness sending a white-hot rush through his blood. Her hands were still cupping his head, her lips still fused with his, her whole body becoming tense and flushing hot. The fire painted her white face gold, made her eyes shine like stars, and then her eyelashes spiked down when his hands swept over her body.

He'd traveled thousands of miles and never found her before. That wonder kept sweeping over him, that he'd accepted loneliness because he thought that was how his life had to be. He'd given up believing there was a woman who matched him, in emotional honesty and temperament, a woman he could be naked with at that rare, elemental soul level.

Her eyes suddenly reopened when he slipped the red sweater over her head. Her hair connected with the angora fabric and crackled with static electricity, caught fire, the same wild-shy fire that was in her eyes.

She liked playing with dynamite. That kind of sheer feminine glow was in her gaze, like, damn, what a shock and surprise to discover that teasing a man to near insanity could be this much fun. They were doing fine, just fine, until she suddenly glanced down and seemed to notice she was half-bare.

His Southern rose, he could have guessed, had magnolia cream skin and the satin swell of firm, full breasts that she'd elected to harness and repress in a good-girl bra. She surely couldn't doubt that he found her beautiful, yet her voice suddenly turned halting and unsure.

"Steve . . . you don't really want this."

A half-second glance below his belt would easily correct *that* misconception, but she happened to be looking straight into his eyes.

"This is just . . . me," she said, as if that announcement might shock him.

He'd heard that tone in her voice before. That I'm-nobody-special-of-course-you're-not-interested-in-*me* tone. It wasn't hard to intuit that she'd been engaged to a son of a sea dog. She must have been hurt deeply, because the lack-of-confidence germ had hold of her like a ruthless flu—but damn. He still couldn't comprehend how she had everything all mixed up. She was special. How could she not know that? She was beautiful and spirited and giving and warm. How could she be so unaware?

Her breath caught when he thumbed open the catch of her bra. Her breasts spilled free, tumbling in his hands, tightening under the slightest touch even though he only meant the tenderest of caresses. He didn't know how to argue with a woman who refused to see reason. The best he knew how to do was show her. Show her what he felt. Show her how he saw her.

Her spine arched when he rubbed his cheek in that valley of soft flesh. Under the reverent stroke of his tongue, the tips hardened to dark rose pearls. He kissed the shadowed hollow of her collarbone. He kissed the velvet spot over her heartbeat. He kissed the underside of each breast, careful to give each equal attention, even more carefully coming back to rewash and dampen those dark pearls with his tongue because, poor baby, she just went crazy when he did that.

In time, his own meticulously slow time, he let his hand drift down over ribs, the downy soft hair on her abdomen, down over her jeans as if the fabric wasn't even there. He cupped the core of her. The fire hissing in the hearth made the same sound as her sudden fretful cry. Her leg tightened around him, and she spun, twisting until she ended up on top of him.

"What are you trying to do to me, Rawlings?"

Her whisper was butter soft and woozy and reeked of frustration. And he'd have answered her question, he really would, but she never gave him the chance. Spread out all over his chest, she kissed him. She took his mouth as volatilely and completely as he'd taken hers. *Geesh.* Just when he was reveling in the role of dominant male, damned if she didn't bedevil him. His she-wolf definitely had claws. And a mind of her own.

His sweater bunched up—her doing—and her fingers conducted a lush exploration of the wiry hair on his chest, a discovery mission that took in muscle shape and skin and, yeah, how frenzied fast his heart was beating. His heater had already been switched on High. She was tempting the risk of a fuse overload, straddling his thighs and rubbing so exquisitely against him. Her lips discovered the shell of his ear—a tickle spot that she couldn't have known—then trailed his jaw and took another heart-slamming, blood-rushing, wildcat claim of a kiss.

He couldn't remember being this miserable. He couldn't remember being this hot, as if he just might die if he couldn't have her. The fever was as carnal and elemental as fire, but lust alone wasn't sending his body temperature over an edge. It was her. Watching her come alive and wild for him, her eyes turning smoky and dark just for him, her touch blind and uninhibitedly sensual and free. Free like he wanted her to feel. With him.

A log crashed in the hearth, sending up fireworks. Her head shot up as if the thumping noise had disoriented her. The look of the whole room suddenly seemed to disorient her, possibly they'd pushed aside the coffee table and rolled right off the rug and were nowhere near where an almost-innocent embrace had started out. Her right hand—the one that had been torturing him with the tease of a finger near the snap of his jeans—suddenly jumped back. And her eyes flew to his with the shock of someone woken from a dream. A fearful dream. Because he swore he saw fear in her eyes.

"Steve...I..."

"Shh. It's all right." He clapped a lid on his desire, or tried to. It was a little like expecting a rattler to quit rattling on command—no way José—but gently he touched her cheek, her hair. If he had no idea what had changed her mood, he didn't need a blueprint to realize it had. "It's all right," he repeated gently. "Nothing's going to happen that you don't want,

Mary. All you ever have to say is no. There's no reason for you to be afraid of anything. Not with me.''

Mary Ellen pried the salt spout open. It was almost
midnight. Samson was polishing glasses behind the
bar. Nearly everyone had gone home except for a few
tables of hard-core rowdies, which gave her the chance
to catch up on housekeeping chores. She unscrewed
the glass pepper shaker and started pouring.

Abruptly she glanced at the shaker and then the row
of shakers she'd been filling down the line of tables.
Geezle beezle. Every single one of the peppers was now
topped with salt. What on earth was she thinking of?

Embarrassment colored her cheeks. Not embarrassment over the spice shakers; that kind of klutzy
mistake was too typical to rate a fuss. The specific
mortification hounding her mind for the past four
days had another source entirely. She rolled her eyes
to the beamed-board ceiling, wishing she could move
to Siberia where she'd never have to face Steve again.

So far, he hadn't come into the bar and she'd successfully avoided his calls through the marvelous in-
vention of the answering machine, but her good luck
couldn't hold forever. Hiding from him struck her as
shamefully adolescent cowardice, but Mary Ellen
didn't particularly care. She'd fallen all over him as if
he were a chunk of Godiva and she was a chocoholic.
She wasn't ready to deal with that. Maybe she'd be
ready to deal with that in the year 2225. Maybe.

She scooped up the row of mixed-up pepper shakers and was hiking for the kitchen when a man's bony
hand yanked on her denim skirt. ''Hey, sweetie pie.
You gonna come home with me tonight?''

Richard Schneider's face registered in her mind. It should; he was the sly-eyed ham-radio owner who'd chased her around her kitchen a few weeks back, but she was just too distracted to worry about him tonight. Without even thinking, she patted his balding head as if he were a small child and moved past.

"Hey! Hey you, darlin'!" he called after her.

"You can have another beer. But not unless you give me your car keys first."

"I wasn't asking you for another beer, and anyway, Samson would give me one without any hassle."

"No, he wouldn't. And you know the rules, dearie dumps. You're at the limit. No car keys, no more."

"Dearie dumps? Did she just call me *dearie dumps?*"

She heard the buzz of guffaws at the table. Vaguely. Pushing through the swinging doors to the grill, she headed for the sink. Samson poked his head around the door, catching her in the act of pouring her salty mistakes down the drain.

"Are you okay?" he asked her.

"Heavens, no. It's been one of those nights when I can't seem to do anything right. I messed up an order, then I broke a glass and then—like a total ditz—I mixed up the peppers and salts—"

"I don't mean anything like that. I mean…are you *feeling* okay?"

"Sure, I'm fine. Why?"

"Why, the lady asks me." Samson started fretfully wiping his hands on a kitchen towel. "Stelmach's out there. You always hide in here by the dishwasher when Stelmach's out there. Fred Claire's had a big table of card players…they've been making dirty jokes at you all night and you haven't bit once. No blushes. No nothing. And you just patted Richy Schneider on the head, made his face turn as red as a beet. Last I knew, you took Richy Schneider's orders from fifteen feet across the room, assuming you were willing to get *that* close, and the lady asks me why I'm wondering if she's okay?''

"Hmm?" She'd started out listening to Samson, but somehow found her concentration wandering to something Steve had told her. Don't show fear around predators or they'll think of you as prey. He'd been talking about wolves, not men, but tarnation. For four days now, she'd been rattled and distracted. For the same four days, the guys in the bar had been angels, nobody giving her any trouble. How startling and annoying to realize he was right. All this time, was that all she had to do? Act unafraid and ignore them, to get those big lugs to behave?

"Mary Ellen, you're not listening to me."

"Of course I'm listening to you, Samson. You're my boss," she said absently. "Speaking of which, I'll close up if you want to go home early. There's hardly anyone here and I can handle it."

"My going home early is *not* what we were discussing."

"Hmm? That's nice, Samson."

For some totally unknown reason, Samson suddenly tossed the towel in the air and muttered something about "*Women,* why even try to understand them?" before disappearing through the swinging doors again. Heaven knew what put the sudden bug in his soup. She finished fixing the pepper shakers, then filled a small bucket with soapy water and headed back into the bar to wash down tables.

Schneider and his group had left, leaving the bar all but empty. She put a shine on the table in the first booth, then moved to the second. For the first time in days, her mind wandered away from Steve and focused on another man entirely.

Johnny. All these months, she mused, she'd been skittery around all men, so afraid of repeating the same judgment mistakes she'd made with him. It struck her, now, how foolish she'd been.

Johnny's face was still clear in her mind—the blond hair and the elegant mouth, the laugh lines around his eyes. No question, she'd believed he was everything she wanted. His family was old-line respectable, no mistake makers or klutzes in the lot, and she'd hoped that kind of stability and acceptance would eventually rub off on her. And Johnny had been a charmer. She'd believed every romantic, seductive word he'd said... and still did. Johnny hadn't lied when he said he loved her. It was just that his idea of love was the champagne rush of seduction. When it came down to commitment, he got cold feet. He was an overgrown boy. But Mary Ellen hadn't known that then, hadn't even come to that conclusion when he stood her up at the altar.

She had to meet a *man* to know what Johnny was.

She had to meet Steve.

She dipped a cloth into the small white bucket, and started scrubbing the third booth. Scrubbing it hard. She'd been so afraid of getting involved with another man like Johnny. What a waste of emotional energy. Now she *knew* what was worth being afraid of... and that was losing her heart on a man—a real man—who couldn't possibly return her feelings.

Steve had been to Alaska. She'd been to Atlanta. Nothing in their life experiences compared. He stood out in a group of men like a giant. If she stood out in a group, it was usually because she had egg on her face. There seemed nothing he couldn't handle. She was a struggler. He was lonely and needed a friend, which undoubtedly affected the chemistry between them, but long-term? The chances of his seriously needing her, Mary Ellen figured conservatively, had to be a million to one.

The telephone rang from the distance behind the bar. Her mind vaguely registered how late it was for a call to be coming in, but Samson answered it. She was busy scouring the table in the last booth. If she rubbed hard enough, maybe she could erase the fantasies from her mind, the memories of how horribly wonderful she'd felt in his arms. She was so good at fixing leaky faucets; how come she couldn't fix her own leaky emotions?

She'd be crazy to believe he cared—she'd been crazy enough to believe in the illusion of love before—but this time her self-respect was on the line. How could she live with herself if she hurt him? It was simply a matter of mind control, of *character,* to be responsible and practical and force herself to think of him only as a friend....

"Mary Ellen," Samson called, "it's for you."

She glanced up. "You mean the telephone call?"

Since Samson was holding out the receiver, it was pretty obvious he meant the telephone call. She just couldn't imagine who would be calling her at work at this late hour. Wiping her damp hands on a towel, she wound her way behind the bar counter and clipped the phone against her ear.

"Hi, love."

Damnation. People used endearments and nicknames around here all the time; even Samson regularly called her "punkin" and "love." But the sound of Steve's husky voice sent a current rippling through her bloodstream as if her whole body had just connected to a soaring electric charge.

"I'm real sorry to call you at work and interrupt you, but I've had a hard time reaching you at home—"

She knew *exactly* why he'd had a hard time reaching her. Samson was looking at her curiously. She whirled around to face the solid row of gleaming glasses, her voice as down low as the fibs that tripped off her tongue. "I'm glad you reached me, because I've been so embarrassed about the other night. I should never have had that wine, Steve. I can't handle wine, never could. Not that that's any excuse, but I didn't want you thinking that I normally behaved that way. I mean . . . you don't have to worry that it would happen again. It was the wine, it wasn't me, and I . . ."

She was about to embellish that whole train of an apology when she heard him sneezing. Not one sneeze. But a series of noisy *serious* sneezes. She forgot about herself. Her forehead pinched in a frown of alarm. "Steve? Are you okay?"

"Not exactly."

"Are you sick?"

"Yeah." Another set of sneezes punctured the conversation. "Which is why I'm calling. Afraid I have a fever. It's damn stupid and annoying—I *never* get sick—but I'm a little wary of taking off cross-country in this weather with a fever this high—"

"Rawlings, you go straight to bed or you're going to hear from me! I swear you men never had the brains you were born with. You don't belong anywhere outside if you have a fever."

"I have to feed the cubs."

She pushed two fingers to her temples. Of course he did. How could she have forgotten his wolf cubs? And those babies were entirely dependent on him.

"There's no one I could ask to help, except for you. I could probably do it. It's just that I'm so dizzy..." He sneezed again. "And weak..." When she said nothing in that instant, he sneezed yet again. "And I seem to be seeing double."

With a sinking sensation, she remembered the day he'd given her his coat. He'd probably caught this cold or flu because of her, crawling around in the snow without adequate protection. And knowing how volatile the wolf issue was in town, she knew he didn't have any backup or help. Unless *she* volunteered.

Hugging the phone tight to her ear, she closed her eyes. "Well, you're not going anywhere outside if you're sick, and that's that. Don't even think about it. I'll be glad to feed them. Just tell me what time their next feeding is supposed to be and where all the formula and everything is."

"Everything's here. At the trailer. And they're going to be real, real hungry around nine tomorrow morning. I hate to ask you—"

"Don't be silly. What are friends for?"

His voice, she noticed, sounded immediately stronger. Apparently he felt that much relief at finding a solution to his problem. But when she hung up the phone, she suddenly couldn't breathe for the helpless hitch in her heartbeat.

She'd just sworn to keep a safe, careful distance from Steve, but this situation was different. He was sick. She'd climb a mountain for him without a qualm if he really needed her. And feeding his pups was no monumental sweat; she'd done it with him enough times so that she knew the procedure.

But had she really just volunteered to face the grown wolves alone?

Seven

Minutes before eight, Steve heard her car door slam. Thankfully he'd anticipated her arriving early. Still, he quickly checked his appearance in the bathroom mirror to make sure he looked appropriately terrible. His oldest navy sweats. Two days' worth of whiskers. Pepper handy, in case he needed to produce sneezing symptoms. He'd been walking around with a heating pad on his neck, which effectively made his face look flushed with fever—but tarnation, he'd forgotten to put away the pad.

He quickly tossed the heating pad in the back of the closet, thinking that looking his absolute worst was a confounded way to woo a woman. On the other hand, desperate men had always been able to justify doing desperate things. His Southern rose had gone to ground ever since the night they'd nearly made love. She'd miraculously never been home when he stopped by, and no message on her answering machine had induced her to return his calls. Nothing had worked . . . until she thought he was ill.

He rumpled his hair just before opening the door—only to earn himself an immediate scolding.

"Get away from that draft, you witless man! I can handle this myself. It's just going to take me a couple of trips."

He should have guessed Red Riding Hood would come armed with goodies. Also that Mary, being Mary, would never suspect sneaky motives in a wolf. Huffing and puffing, she set a huge pot on his stove—from the incredible smell, it was homemade chicken soup—then hustled back out to bring in a sack of supplies.

"I don't know if you need a doctor. I figured we'd cross that bridge when we came to it. But in the meantime, I didn't want you to have to go out for stuff, so I brought O.J. and antihistamines and aspirin and a thermometer. . . ." As she verbally cataloged all the supplies, her hood slipped back, revealing softly tousled mink brown hair and cheeks pinkened from the cold. She quickly ripped off her gloves and brushed the back of her hand to his forehead and neck. "Oh, Lord, Steve, you're so hot."

"I know," he said pitifully.

A bossy forefinger waggled in front of his nose. "Well, I'm putting you to bed. Right now. And I don't want to hear any arguments."

"Yes, ma'am."

"We'll draw the shades and get you set up with a drink and some aspirin. You can be flat on your back and still tell me how to fix the recipe for the formula. There is *nothing* you have to worry about, Steve. Once

I've got the bottles ready, I'll drive my car to exactly the same place you always park your truck. I know how to find the wolves' den from there, and I've fed the babies enough times with you so I know how it's done. Everything'll go fine. In fact, I'll be back here before you know it.''

Through this whole monologue, she herded him back into the bedroom and supervised his climbing into bed. She pulled up the sheet and comforter, added the Hudson Bay blanket, then wasn't happy until she found and added an afghan to the covers. "Are you warm enough?" she said, worried.

A snake couldn't be hotter in the tropics. "I'm fine," he said weakly. "And thanks."

"Poor baby. You look so miserable."

"I've felt better," he said bravely.

"Flus are awful, aren't they?" She patted and fussed and tucked, then abruptly stopped. By then he was reasonably sure he had a legitimate fever. Through all those covers, she'd been patting and tucking some meaningful body parts. Possibly she realized that, too, because suddenly she skidded back with a flustered shine on her cheeks. "Now be honest. Have you had a problem being sick to your stomach? Diarrhea? Because I have no way of knowing if you need medicine for certain things unless you tell me."

"Good grief. No!"

Mary Ellen had extraordinarily deep, soulful, melting-soft eyes. Just then, though, they had an army general's shrewdness. "Now don't wimp out on me, Rawlings. We're both adults. Everybody's had those embarrassing kinds of flus. Are you telling me the truth?"

"Yes. Honest to Henry. Yes."

"Well...okay then. I'll get started on the pups' formula."

It took her twenty minutes to get the pups' formula blended, the bottles organized and her snow gear donned. The instant her car left the driveway, Steve bounded out of bed.

It was clearly dangerous to be ill around that woman, it was a mistake he never intended to make again, but so far, his plan was coming fine. Never mind about honor and honesty. He'd had to do *something* to get her to talk with him again. As he could have guessed, neither hell, high water nor combustible sexual chemistry was going to stand in that lady's way if she thought someone needed her. She was natural and easy with him again. Exactly what he'd hoped.

But that never meant he had any intention of leaving her alone with the wolves.

He drove the truck, taking a backwoods route different from hers, then hiked on snowshoes toward the den site. Binoculars were stuffed in his pocket, his tranq gun swinging from a strap on his shoulder. He'd never have let Mary Ellen go—at all—if he anticipated there being a problem. The wolves knew her now, had accepted her around the pups. Still, carrying the tranquilizer gun was insurance. And being no farther than twenty feet from her was a guarantee she could take to the bank, even if she didn't know it.

He installed himself in the shadowy arms of a big, fat, maternal spruce located on the ridge top. There was no way to travel at breakneck speed on snowshoes, but as he'd expected, he arrived before her. Mary Ellen not only hiked at a woman's pace, but she was slowed down by all the feeding gear.

Behind him, yards away, he heard the almost inaudible crunch of footsteps in snow. The wolves. The slugabeds must have been feeling lazy this morning, because he'd expected to hear them long before this. Waiting for Mary Ellen, he had ample time to clean the lens on his binoculars. Time, too, to feel the nagging assault of guilt on his conscience.

By Steve's code of ethics, a good man never forced a woman to do something she was afraid of. Mary was afraid of the wolves. And afraid of him. No matter what happened on that snuggly plush rug in front of her fire, any idiot could figure out that she hadn't wanted to see him since. It was her right to make that decision and that choice, and a guy who messed with that was being a manipulative horse's behind.

But damn. How could he "roll-over-Beethoven" when they were as good together as fire and flint? She'd reached him from the start with her humor and understanding and warmth, and she plugged straight into his heart, the way she came alive in his arms. His whole life had switched on like a light-bulb-glow of possibilities since she'd been in it. They weren't just good together. They were potentially unforgettable together, but so far, it had been an uphill job to get Mary Ellen to notice the grass right under their feet.

He suspected that son of a sea dog was the source of the bullet in her confidence, but guessing that was no help. She closed up on the subject of her ex-fiancé. Steve couldn't force her to believe in her feelings and trust him. But he'd definitely noticed that every time he pushed his delicate Southern rose off a cliff—when he didn't lift a finger to help her—she seemed to gain faith in herself. Faith in her own strength, faith in her own judgment.

Maybe this time was different, though.

Shoot, maybe this time was doomed to be a disaster.

He spotted her red hood, bouncing down the slope from the crest of the ravine. And he heard her voice, even before she reached the clearing and started organizing gear. Initially the sound of her voice made him grin. She was talking to the wolves, echoing exactly what he did, using a quiet, calm tone to let the animals identify where she was. Only the nature of her monologue was a little different than what he would have used.

"All right, y'all. You know I'm here. I know I'm here. Everybody knows I'm here, so y'all can just go back to napping and forget all about me, you hear? We're all just gonna stay real cool about this— *Damn!*"

Steve's shoulders hunched forward, his attention riveted on White Wolf. The other times she'd been around, the big white had never taken his eyes off her. Steve empathized with the alpha male's fascination, since he shared an identical obsession with the lady himself, and he knew his old friend. White Wolf was fully capable of being a gentleman around a lady, and always before, he'd kept his distance.

Not this time. The other wolves in the pack stood alert, located on the same high level of ridge as Steve, as if their leader had given the command to stay back. But White Wolf hurled down the ravine in a streak of silvery-sunlit fur and padded straight for the entrance to the den, blocking it, facing Mary Ellen with his big, white, gorgeous sharp teeth noticeably barred.

"Oh, spit. Oh, shoot. Oh, damn. I think I'm gonna throw up," Mary Ellen crooned.

Without making a sound, Steve slid the tranq gun from its leather strap and aimed it.

"Now listen, sweetie pie, I understand how you feel. I'm one of those rotten humans," Mary Ellen continued in the same soft, seductive Southern drawl. "Why should you trust me, hmm? Hells bells, I don't even trust me. I've screwed up my life in ways you can't even imagine, lovebug, but there comes a time when a woman simply has to take a stand. I mean, if she takes off running every time there's a tough problem, her self-respect goes straight down the tubes. Try to understand. I'm not going down that road again, not even for you. Which means, I'm afraid, that I'm not running and somehow the two of us are gonna have to make friends. Come here."

The whole nature of that soft feminine monologue momentarily mesmerized Steve, until he saw her pull off a glove and extend the back of her slim, white hand. Adrenaline slammed his pulse into high gear. The last thing, the absolute *last* thing, she needed to do was approach that wolf in any way that he could misconstrue as aggressive. He'd ingrained that lesson into her from her first encounter with the critters. She *knew* better.

"Come on. You heard me, darling. Come on over here. You can smell the food. You've smelled that milk on your pups before, haven't you? But if you can't figure out that I'm a friend, then you're just going to have to come here and smell me, too. Quit that stupid growling and come on, baby. Come on, love..."

White Wolf whined and pawed, clearly disturbed by the human's unexpected behavior. The big wolf wasn't alone. Driveling sweat suddenly itched the back of Steve's neck. His stomach was tightening in knots and his finger was braced steady, steady on the trigger for the tranq gun.

He saw the wolf cock his head, then pace uneasily, restlessly, toward her. He saw, but he didn't believe, when the wolf's long snout hesitantly sniffed her slim, white, too-damn vulnerable hand. His palms were so slick with sweat that his finger slipped off the trigger. Or maybe that was shock. Because with his own eyes, he saw White Wolf's tongue snake out and wash her hand.

"That's a boy, that's a boy. Well, aren't you a lover. I'd about die before hurting you or your babies. You just had to figure that out, didn't you? You want to come with me while I feed your pups?"

It was nearly noon before Mary Ellen got back to the trailer. She hesitated at the door, unwilling to barge in unannounced, but not wanting to knock and risk waking Steve if he'd managed to fall asleep.

When she quietly stepped inside, though, she found Steve not only awake, but midstride to pacing the length of his trailer. In that first instant, she didn't catch a look at his face. "How are you feeling?"

"To be honest—like someone swept the rug out from under me."

"Well, that's to be expected with a fever." She slid all the feeding supplies onto the counter, then hustled out of her coat and snow gear.

"The fever broke. I'm fine."

As if she'd take his word for it. She raised on tiptoe to lay her wrist against his forehead. "Well, I'll be darned. You do feel cool. Actually you feel almost cold…" She rocked back on her heels, trying to study him objectively. It wasn't easy. Certainly he looked different with his wildly rumpled hair and the roguish whiskers on his chin, but the masculine glint in his eyes seemed as clear and intense as ever, and his old sweats molded intimately over every male muscle and bone.

He looked better sick than a thousand men would look healthy. His color was natural, and his mouth... her pulse ricocheted when she found herself, embarrassingly, staring at his mouth. There was a hint of a crooked grin on the devil's mouth that she didn't quite understand, and when she glanced up, there were the devil's eyes waiting for her, as if he saw something in her face that her own mirror didn't. No wonder she felt unsettled. "Your fever *must* have dropped if you're this cool," she said again.

He moved past the subject of his health as if it never existed. "How'd it go?" he asked impatiently.

"You mean, how'd it go with the wolves? Great. I couldn't believe how much the pups had grown in just the few days since I'd seen them. They're so active. And so endearingly clumsy. They're moving around. Two of them have even made it to the outside of the den."

"You didn't have any trouble with White Wolf? Or any of the other adults?"

"Heavens, no." She moved swiftly toward the sink, thinking she'd ladle out some of the chicken soup she'd brought earlier. If he was feeling better, he needed food to build his strength. She wasn't about to tell Steve of those few terror-clutching moments when White Wolf had confronted her. He respected her competence; he'd assumed she had the ability to handle his babies was fine or he'd never have asked her to go. How could she tell him that she'd almost run for the hills and almost, badly, let him down when he needed her?

"Then nothing special happened to scare you?"

"Scared? Me? Now, just sit at the counter while I get you some soup. Trust me, the noodles are to die for. My mom always made them from scratch and they're nothing like the tasteless stuff that comes out of a package.... *Why* are you smiling at me, Rawlings?"

"Maybe because you keep doing things to make me smile."

Like what, she wanted to ask him, but was too scared to risk hearing the answer. They were doing fine—they'd done fine from the beginning—as long as she put a lock on her hormones and emotions and just acted the part that she wanted to be: a friend. An honest, simple, old, basic friend.

She finished a bowl of soup, then cupped a palm under her chin and watched him dive for seconds—and then thirds. "You're definitely feeling better," she said with relief.

"I told you."

"I know. But men never tell the truth when they're sick. You're all usually impossible-to-handle monsters. Worse than small children. Can't trust a word you say."

"Hey." But he chuckled at her teasing, and reached for another piece of crusty French bread. "I'm still weak and need some company."

"Hah. You just want me to stay and do the dishes. And you should have called me before this if you were sick. I'd always be glad to help with the pups."

"You still haven't said much about that. Everything really went as smooth as silk this morning? Are you sure nothing happened that you want to tell me about?''

What could she tell him? That a six-foot terrifying wolf had completely stolen her heart? That, too damn much like Steve, he was courageous and strong and she knew—she *knew*—that big white wolf had the power to hurt her. Yet there was an aloneness she sensed in both male animals. A loneliness, and a hunger for affection and caring, that just kept sabotaging her logical instincts about staying away and avoiding danger.

Those same logical instincts made her pick up her coat right after doing the dishes. More one-on-one contact with Steve was distinctly, recognizably unsafe. She meant to leave, but somehow it didn't happen. She bossed the big lug into lying on the couch with an afghan, but no way was he obeying orders about taking a nap and resting. Every time she made motions to leave, he brought up something else. They ended up talking about psychological suspense books, and international trade agreements, and how they both loved mountains, and how Samson and his wife had ever gotten together, and yeah, inevitably the conversation drifted to wolves.

"What comes next with the cubs?" she asked him. "I mean, they're growing so fast. How do you feed them after they move past the bottle stage?"

"They're coming to that interim stretch right now. They're hungry for more than milk, but not quite ready for solid food. Not to gross you out, but if their mama were alive, what she'd do is overeat, then regurgitate that chewed-up meal for them."

"Yuck." She squinched her nose at the mental picture. "I give—how are you going to manage *that?*"

"Not quite like their mama," Steve said dryly. "I'll just use that blender you thankfully fixed and gradually add raw meat to the milk mixture. There'll come a point where it won't be a problem, because the whole pack will start helping me. They're a family. And in a pack family, everyone takes on the job of feeding the young."

"You mean everybody throws up for the babies?"

He grinned again. "Yup. Doesn't sound too appealing, does it, but the system works for them. Considering how much full-time work the babies make, it's probably a good thing there's only one litter in a pack. Although I'm not sure the boy wolves would agree with me on that point. I've told you why there's only one litter, haven't I? That the alpha male is the only one who gets to mate?"

"Yes, but I thought you were kidding. You mean none of the other guys get to fool around? White Wolf's the only one who gets a girl?"

"That's right. He chooses his lady—the best lady, the strongest and prettiest and sexiest she-wolf around. And once he picks a mate, that's it. She's his. And nobody, but nobody else, had better dare touch his girl."

She opened her mouth with another question—she'd been having a great time with the whole conversation—yet suddenly her mind couldn't conjure up a single coherent thought. Steve was looking at her. Stretched on the couch, a pillow stuffed behind his neck, he couldn't appear more lazy or relaxed. There was just something in those deep, dark cobalt eyes that unnerved her. White Wolf, that morning, had studied her the same way... until he made his move.

Steve wasn't making any "moves." There was no reason to feel this sudden lunge of emotion, this crazy sensation that she was neck deep in trouble and didn't know it. Her imagination was simply triggered by the kindred spirit between those two. Like White Wolf, she sensed that when Steve claimed a mate, that'd be it. She'd be his. He took all those primitive, archaic values about honor and loyalty seriously, and his whole nature was protective. Mary Ellen had no doubt that Steve would be there on a dime if anyone dared touch—or harm—a lady he loved.

There was nothing in that whole thought train to make her nervous. Yet her heart suddenly thumped like a mad dog's tail when Steve slowly, quietly, swung his legs over the side of the couch.

"It suddenly occurred to me," he said, "how tired you must be."

"I'm not the least tired," she said swiftly.

"No? You worked late last night, probably couldn't have gotten to bed before two. And you must have been up at daybreak, to make that soup and be over here to help me. And then you were with the cubs all morning."

"It was nothing. Any friend would have done the same thing." She was curled up in his easy chair with her legs tucked, and she saw him step toward her, even saw him bend down. Another lunge of electricity charged through her pulse—which she repressed. Where was her brain? His similarity to the big alpha male couldn't be more comforting. When Steve got around to choosing a mate, he would undoubtedly choose the strongest and prettiest and sexiest she-wolf around, simply because anything less than special wouldn't suit him at all. Mary Ellen was as ordinary as chicken soup, which he surely knew by now. She was safe. She was sure.

"Friends help each other," Steve agreed. "But that doesn't mean I don't owe this particular friend a thank-you."

"Heavens, you don't owe me anything—"

Apparently he was convinced otherwise. He cocked his head. In the next second, she felt his lips, warm and supple, moving over hers. It was only the brush of a kiss, the feather of a connection, a gift and no taking implied . . . or it started that way.

A clock ticked somewhere. His refrigerator hummed. Watery winter sunlight shone through his trailer windows, plain old sunlight, nothing magical. Yet her lips clung to his, as if they'd hungered for another taste of him. And her hands found their way around his neck, as if they'd been yearning to hold him for all this time.

She really knew there was no magic. It was just like a season of hot, humid weather in Georgia. There was no relief, not from the ripening explosion of emotion she felt for him, nor in all the foolish yearnings he aroused. She thought: I'm going to catch his cold. She thought: I don't give a damn.

She'd sampled his flavor of passion before. The flavor was wild, dangerous, compelling, and one of these days he was bound to discover the real Mary Ellen. She doubted he would respect that lady, doubted he would be attracted to the failure-and-mistaken-ridden woman she really was, but just then she wanted to keep those guilty secrets a little longer. No man, ever, had made her feel this way. Like climbing Everest would be snap. Like her whole slate was clean and she could do anything, be any woman she wanted, when she was with him.

Slowly he lifted his head. His skin was golden in the light, his eyes a silvery dark blue and like a mirror on her face. "I never expected to find a ... friend ... like you."

"I ..." It struck her as a superb idea to talk about being friends. It was just tricky to talk at all when her bones were still jelly and her heart was still spinning.

"It's never been easy for me to ask anyone for help," Steve admitted.

"Me, either."

"I thought you'd understand." His grin came slow. Just as slowly as the strand of hair he pushed, gently, caressingly, from her brow. "We're a matched pair of misfits, aren't we? Us stubborn independent types need to stick together."

Later, on the drive home, that conversation replayed in her mind like a jammed tape. She seemed to have agreed to something, but she wasn't sure what. That they were friends? That two cussedly independent people naturally stuck together? That they could count on each other for help?

In her driveway, she cut the engine and pressed a palm to her temples. Everything was fine, she told herself. She *wanted* Steve to feel that he could count on her. She *wanted* to be that gutsy, strong, self-reliant woman he believed was his friend.

She just didn't want to make a fool out of herself again. Johnny had irrevocably taught her how susceptible she was to the illusion of love. Her self-respect had nose-dived to the pits over that mistake, and it had been a blunder-bust job to win it back. Steve was lonely. He was also an affectionate and passionately caring man.

She simply needed to be careful not to confuse that reality with what it wasn't.

Love.

Eight

"**I** knew I should have made you stay home."

"*Tch-tch*. We have to do something about the archaic ideas you have about women, Rawlings. You can't make us do anything these days. Haven't you heard?"

Steve only stopped walking long enough to yank the hood protectively over her head. Her teasing clearly wasn't getting through. His scowl was as broody as a dark thundercloud. "I should have," he muttered again, "made you stay home. You're already wet. And cold. If I'd had a brain, I'd have tied you to a chair by a nice warm fireplace."

"You could have tried," she said demurely.

"Good grief. Is that *more* sass coming from the peanut gallery?"

She chuckled. "I wanted to come, remember? I volunteered. You think I wanted to stay home and miss all this?'' She feigned a look of awe for the landscape around them. ''I don't think I've ever seen a more perfect day for mud wrestling.''

Steve rolled his eyes, but then he laughed. He cuffed her shoulder in a quick companionable squeeze, and then they trudged on. Or slogged on, Mary Ellen thought wryly.

A week ago, the whole countryside had been a fairyland of emerald pines and white satin snow. Every day the woods had been priceless, a fresh treasure to explore. But who could anticipate Michigan weather? Faster than a finger snap, the temperature started warming. Instead of snow, the sky started dripping drizzle. The snow melted in dirty gray chunks. And beneath the snow, the ground was as slippery as a mud slide.

Steve hadn't asked for help. She could have stayed home by that nice warm fire he kept bringing up. She'd already fallen twice. The seat of her snow pants was muddy, so were her gloves, and crashing in a graceless heap—twice yet—in front of Steve had been embarrassing. There was nothing glamorous or fun about sloshing through mud so thick it sucked at her boots and threatened her balance at every knoll.

More relevant to Mary Ellen, she'd warned herself a dozen times to be careful, to limit her one-on-one time with Steve. But heavens. Neither kisses nor closeness was conceivably a worry in this situation. Carting the food supplies for the cubs had been marginally easy with a sled. Without snow, the sled was useless. The cubs were bigger now, which meant there was more food to carry. And Steve would have had to backpack it all in alone if she hadn't volunteered to help.

Once they reached the valley, she automatically scanned the crest of the ridge for the sentinels. Thunder, the light gray, typically let out a brave howl from behind the safe distance of a tree. Scarlett was parading back and forth, making sure everyone knew she was there, and Hamlet was prancing on the ridge edge. It took Mary Ellen a second to realize that one shadow was missing. "Where's White Wolf?"

Steve, just behind her, had paused to check out their greeting party, too. "I'm sure he's around. Just not in sight."

A trickle of alarm caused her heart to race. Always before, White Wolf had been visibly out front and ahead of his pack. Still, when her gaze flew to Steve's face, she saw no frown of worry or concern. He knew the big white's behavior better than she did, and feeling reassured, she forgot that momentary instinct of alarm. It was only minutes later that they both had their hands full.

The cubs were waiting for them outside the den. Her darling babies, she thought ruefully, had turned into monsters. Their ears were perky now; their eyes were changing color from that soft birth blue to gold and brown. None of them had an ounce of patience; their appetites were rapacious; and though they were still clumsy and unsteady, they'd discovered fighting. Their fine woolly fur was a damp muddy mess because they'd all been rolling in the muck.

"They're practicing to see who's going to end up dominant," Steve told her.

"That might be a high-class ethologist theory. Personally I think that particular behavior crosses all species lines. It has nothing to do with wolves—it has to do with males. Boys like to play in the mud. It's a universal truth.''

''You think it's just a guy thing, hmm?'' Steve scratched his chin. ''I was going to suggest that you stay back. You know, let me feed 'em, so you could stay clean. But I see you're already on your knees and in the middle of the muck—''

''Hey, I didn't come all this way just to watch from the sidelines.''

''I haven't seen you do anything yet from the sidelines. But keep your gloves on, okay?''

She kept her gloves on. She already knew the cubs had sharp claws, and the little devils-in-training played rough. Steve had rules about limiting their physical contact with the babies. The less they bonded with people, the safer they would be surviving later in the wild. Bottle-feeding required a certain closeness, but the minute they were old enough to stand steady, the milk and meat mixture was poured into a dish. The dish scene was still new, and the cubs considered it an excuse for a free-for-all, each sibling nuzzling and growling and bickering for his share. Any innocent human body trying to refill the dish risked being trampled in the battlefield.

''Listen, you doofuses. You guys could use a lesson from the human concept of taking turns. There's enough for everybody, haven't y'all figured that out by now? Honestly, I— Steve, what's wrong?''

''Nothing.''

Sure there was. She sensed rather than saw Steve suddenly jerk to his feet. Temporarily her head was down as she spoon-poured the last of the pups' meal, and it took a second to extricate herself from the scramble of baby bodies. When she stood up, she saw

Steve crouched down several yards away, his right glove off, his palm raised to his nose to sniff something. He lurched to his feet abruptly.

"I want you to stay here with the pups for a couple of minutes, okay?" he asked her.

Positively, she had no gift for reading his mind, never had, but her feminine radar had fine-tuned a private channel for his moods. She'd heard that calm, lazy tone before. Throw a tornado at Steve, and he automatically dropped to slow gear, a technique that effectively calmed everyone around him. Except for her. "What did you find in the snow?"

"Nothing I'm sure of. Everything's fine. I just want to check out something. I won't be far."

He was correct about that, because she was right behind him. She sidetracked to the slushy mound of snow that first caught his attention, and was momentarily mystified. Dirty snow was dirty snow; it all looked the same... until she noticed the odd-colored brown spots. They were really more brown than red, so there was no reason for her to associate them with blood. If White Wolf hadn't been missing. And Steve hadn't suddenly turned so calm, cool and quiet.

Her lungs were heaving by the time she caught up with him. He'd climbed the ridge with far more grace—and far less noise—than she could manage. When she reached the top, he'd stopped dead. He was wiping the matted rain from his face, but his blue eyes pinned her. "I should have known you'd figure out what I was doing. But you're not coming with me. You're going straight back to the cubs."

"No, I'm not."

"An injured wolf is nothing to mess with. If he's hurt, he's mean. Forget any friendship or good feelings he formed toward humans. They won't apply. He'll probably attack anyone or anything that tries to get near him."

"All the more reason why you need someone with you. If he's injured badly, it could take two of us to handle him."

"It might. But since you're not going to handle him—or go anywhere near him—that won't be a problem."

"I'm coming with you."

"Over my dead body."

Who would have guessed those sleepy, seductive blues could turn colder than steel? But she lifted her chin. "You can argue all you want. I'm not leaving you."

"Dammit, Mary." He ran a hand through his hair. "When you get married, the guy's gonna have a helluva shock if he tries to put 'obey' in the service. And I don't have *time* to make you see reason—"

"Trust me. It'd be a worthless exercise."

She was hoping for a smile. Instead she got an index finger waggling in her face. *"Stay behind me."*

She followed behind him, trudging through brush and sludgy mud for another half mile, miserably aware that he was mad at her but unable to see how she could make any other choice. She knew how much he loved that wolf. She *knew*. No matter how scared she was about what they were going to find, how could she desert him to face it alone?

Her right foot cramped. Rain dribbled down her temples and nape. No matter how skilled Steve was at finding tracks and signs, the weather inhibited his progress, too. She could see the strain of worry in the tight lines around his mouth.

As they trudged another half mile, Steve explained that if the wolf sensed he was weak enough to attract predators, the animal's first instinct would be to distance himself as far from the den as possible. Mary Ellen understood what that meant—the damn wolf would be determined to travel, even if he was injured, *because* he was injured. The instinct to protect his pack and young, in her view, was unforgivably stupid. Nature was stupid. She'd always had complete respect for nature and nature's laws, until that unbearable instant when they rounded a tangled thicket of grapevines and she saw the still, white mound hidden in the boughs of a huge pine.

Steve hustled straight for the wolf. For a moment, she couldn't. Her heart slammed in her chest. The lump in her throat was big enough to make her sick. She'd never stopped, entirely, being scared of the big lug, but he was magnificent and wonderful and she loved him and if he were dead . . . Oh, God, if he were dead.

Steve suddenly spun around and saw her face. "Aw, honey. Don't look like that. If he managed to travel this far, I'm betting he can't be hurt that badly."

"I was just thinking the same thing." She'd lied to him a zillion times. What was one more?

His knuckles brushed her cheek. "Are you okay?"

"Of course I'm okay." She swallowed that horrible lump and said thickly, "Whatever you have to do, I'll help."

He wasn't dead. When Steve pushed off his backpack and knelt down beside him, White Wolf opened his eyes and lunged. His sharp teeth barely missed Steve by inches, yet Mary Ellen tasted the sweet flavor of relief that at least he was alive. Her eyes caught the dull glint of metal in the shadows. Gray silver metal. Steve had undoubtedly known from the tracks that the wolf was carrying a steel-jawed trap on his paw, but she had no idea.

When Steve saw the bloody mess, he swore low and long and soothingly. Once he started crooning to the White Wolf, he never stopped. Mary Ellen never had time to think after that; there was too much to do.

"We'll get that off, pal, you're going to be fine, just fine. Mary, open the backpack, will you? There's a small plastic box . . . stay still, fella, just stay still."

"Is his foot broken?"

"I'm hoping nothing's broken, but I'm not sure yet."

As soon as she handed him the plastic box, he cracked it open. She saw an array of medicine and hypodermics. "Can you give him something for pain?"

"I know it sounds cruel, love, but we don't want to use anything like that unless we have to. He's in shock, aren't you, big guy? Depressants are dangerous if he's in shock, so we're going to start with an antibiotic and then just see if there's a prayer he'll behave when I take off that trap. You gonna be a good boy for me? Sure you are. . . . Just empty the tools from the bottom of the pack on the ground, Mary, everything. Damned if I know how we're going to get that bastard off, but we'll just have to find a way. We've known each other a long time, haven't we, pal? Remember how I found your mama, in an illegal trap just like this? Well, nothing like that is going to happen to you, because you're gonna be fine, but you have to let me get to it, fella. Put your head down. Put your head down, that's a boy."

The temperature dropped. The drizzly rain turned to sleet that stung her face and froze her toes. Steve could swear in four languages, she discovered, and though he never raised his voice above a singsong mellow croon, he discussed with White Wolf, in precise detail, finding the man who'd used the illegal trap and exactly what he'd like to do to him.

A half hour passed, maybe an hour, maybe more than an hour. The constant pump of adrenaline and anxiety made time blur. Even after the trap was removed, the wound cleaned and bandaged, Mary Ellen knew they weren't free to rest yet. They still had to collect all the feeding supplies for the cubs, then hike back to the truck in this sleety mudfest, and she had no idea what he was going to do with White Wolf after this.

Still, there was an in-between moment, when Steve had done all he could with the emergency supplies from his pack, and he crawled out from under the tree to stand up and stretch. He was a mess, hatless, his hair matted down and damp, dirt crusted all over him, and a long smudge of mud on his jaw. "He'll be okay. Not today, not tomorrow, either, but he'll be okay."

She guessed that, knew it, from the look in his eyes. Steve loved that wolf. Fiercely. She'd known those two were spiritual brothers before, but her heart still clutched in awe at his handling of the animal. He'd wooed a trust and gentleness that should never have existed between man and wolf. Still, his slow smile now was added reassurance that White Wolf was really going to be all right.

"I hate to tell you this, short stuff, but you really look like hell."

"Me? Good thing we don't have a mirror around here, Rawlings. You'd scare yourself if you got a look."

"Yeah?" He glanced down, then back at her. "I think the mud definitely looks better on you. Good thing, too, since you seem to be wearing most of the topsoil in this forest."

"Hey."

He chuckled, but his boyish grin slowly faded. His complete concentration had been on the wolf all this time; how could it possibly be otherwise? Yet his gaze suddenly homed in on her face, as if she'd been on his mind, as if he'd never been less than aware of her at his side. "You're one hell of a trooper, Mary."

His praise, his quiet respect, made her cheeks glow. She shook her head swiftly. "I'm not a trooper. I've never been a trooper. I didn't do anything—"

"Yeah, you did, and yeah, you are. One of these days, I'm going to have to find some way to make you believe it."

Mary Ellen's head was wrapped in a towel when she heard the knock on the door. She tore the towel off with a startled glance at the bedroom clock. It was barely five. Steve wasn't due for dinner until seven. She'd just yanked on an old pair of sweats; her feet were bare and her hair still wet from the shower.

She'd strangle him if he showed up this early.

That murderous thought train didn't last long. Her heart was chugging anticipation as she jogged for the door. They'd been impossibly busy this past week. Steve had carried White Wolf out of the woods and created a nest for him close to the pups. The wolf was recovering fast—he'd been on his feet for two days now—but Steve had a full plate between feeding the pack and the added time of caring for the injured animal. The trapper had added an extra problem. Steve had contacted the authorities about the illegal trap, but no one had been caught. Steve spent every spare minute patrolling the forested area around the den, worried the jerk might try to set other traps or do something else to harm his wolves.

She'd helped him. Who else could have? She'd worked beside him as close as a hand and glove, knowing she was being reckless, and knowing she was courting even more danger when she'd asked him for dinner tonight. He'd been catching all his meals on the run. He needed rest and real food. She wasn't being an idiot and counting on any future; she wasn't even dreaming nonsense like that, but being there for him when he needed help...*damn*, it felt good. This whole week, she'd felt higher than a soaring kite, as if she was hugging a secret no one could take away from her.

With a burst of a smile, she pulled open the door.

Her smile didn't disappear. It just froze. Her disappointment was unreasonable; she had no reason to think Steve would be able to break away and come early. But she'd rather entertain a grizzly on her front porch than this particular visitor. Giles Labeck was one of the single-guy cronies in Fred Claire's crowd. Typically he was dressed in a hunter's jacket and combat boots. Just as typically, he looked her over with a bulldog's fondness for a chew toy.

"Hi there, Mary Ellen."

"Hi there, yourself. What can I do for you?" But one uneasy glance told her why he was here—he was carrying a six-pack under one arm, and a VCR with dangling cords under the other.

"My machine's on the blink. Thought I'd give you a shot at fixing it before going to all the trouble of sending it in."

Aw hell, she thought gloomily. She could hardly build up a business by turning away customers, and truthfully she had ample time to dress and make dinner before seven. It was just...Giles. She'd rather spend time with a rattler, and would certainly trust the snake a lot more. "Well...come in. I've got a pretty heavy work schedule, but I'll give it a look. It should only take a couple of minutes to be able to tell you if it's something I can handle or not."

"Well, that's no sweat, darlin'. I've got all evening."

She could have guessed that, from the way he dropped his jacket and settled in. Judging from the teensy red lines in his eyes, he'd made inroads into a few beers already, but she warned herself not to jump to conclusions.

"I heard you've become real good friends with the wolf man." Giles motioned with a can of beer. When she shook her head, he popped one open for himself.

"Steve? Yes, we're friends." Ignoring Mr. Leering-Eyes, she bent down to plug in his VCR and make the connections.

"He's sure raising a ruckus about that trap. Got the game warden, the sheriff, everybody and his uncle riled up. Foolishness, in my book. People been trapping in this area for two centuries. Anybody could have had one of those old-fashioned traps in their family from years back, ain't no way to pin down who it belonged to. And a man's got a right to protect his family from wolves."

"The trap was on state forest land. Nobody's private property. Nor was the wolf near anyone's home or backyard. And there are reasons that kind of trap was outlawed years ago. You think it's okay to maim an animal and then leave it to die?"

Giles chuckled, then hunkered down beside her. "Ain't hard to figure out whose side you're on." He paused. "He's a big guy, isn't he? Guess it ain't too hard to understand why you find him appealing. A little thing like you, living all alone on these long winter nights...."

"Hmm. What's wrong with the VCR? What's it doing?"

"I get white fuzz at the top of the screen. Sometimes it clears up and sometimes it don't. You like a big man, do you, honey?"

Ignoring chicken pox didn't make the symptoms disappear, but Mary Ellen gave it a lion's try. She hadn't been through any awkward, embarrassing scenes in weeks now. She'd really hoped that her mortifying habit of landing herself in sticky messes was long gone. And her glance kept straying to the window. What would Steve think of her, if he walked in and found this dimwit chasing her around the living room?

It took some time to make the connections and test the machine, but she was thorough. If she could fix and finish the problem right now, Giles wouldn't have any excuse for coming back. "When exactly do you get this fuzz? When you first put in a tape, after it's been running a while, when?"

"She just does it sporadiclike. No rhyme or reason."

"You're sure it's not just old tapes you're putting in? Because I'm not finding any problem with the machine...Giles, for some unknown reason, your hand is on my knee. If you want to stay alive, I suggest you move it in the next two seconds."

"You got such a cute sense of humor."

"Thank you. Remove your hand," she repeated.

"Hey, now. You don't have to be so unfriendly. We're not strangers. You think I couldn't show you a real good time? Nothing wrong with a couple of people getting together on a lonely winter night—"

"There's nothing wrong with your VCR," she said wearily.

"Maybe not, but I sure got a problem you could fix real, real easy—"

"Read my lips, Giles. *No*. It's not a two syllable word. You shouldn't have all that much trouble understanding it." She quickly unplugged and disconnected his machine, but while she was bent down, she felt his beefy hand trail down her spine. "Shoot," she said irritably, and spun around with the screwdriver in her hand.

"Now, darlin'—" He saw the screwdriver.

"How come being nice doesn't work? It works for other people all the time. How come, would you answer me that, I have to get mean when I absolutely *hate* getting mean? Is there some sign on my forehead that says Mary Ellen is a patsy?"

"Sign? You're confusing me, honey, I don't know what you're talking about. What sign?"

"Forget the sign. Concentrate, Giles, on the door. You're leaving." She poked him in the chest with the screwdriver. "Take your VCR. And your beer." She poked him again. "Right now."

Ousting him brought back shades of old nightmares, memories of feeling foolish and guiltily miserable for never handling problems like this well, but she had no time to dwell on it. She caught a look at the clock. To get everything done before Steve arrived was going to take some fancy footwork.

Running around the kitchen faster than a mad dog, she dredged the chicken in crackers and Parmesan cheese, started it frying and then zipped back to the bedroom to pull on a green tunic sweater and stirrups. She set the table, turned the chicken, then raced back to the bedroom to put on makeup and do her hair. It was later, when she tossed the salad and pushed her poppyseed Swiss bread into the oven, that she recalled the look on Giles's face when he stumbled over his own combat boots. He'd looked so silly. A chuckle bubbled in her throat, and turned into a peal of laughter.

Slowly that laughter faded, but inside, deep inside, Mary Ellen was conscious of something strange happening. Even a month ago, she wouldn't have laughed at herself, would never have seen any humor in the situation. Even weeks ago, she'd have been anxious to the point of tongue-tied nerves with a handful like Labeck. Now she'd been annoyed more than shook up. And maybe she'd handled him clumsily, but she *had* handled him.

"You're a trooper," Steve had told her.

She hadn't believed him. Thinking of herself as a failure-prone doofus had become so ingrained that it never occurred to her that she really wasn't the same woman who'd left Georgia. She'd let Steve think things about her courage and self-reliance that had no remote connection to truth. Somehow, though, in trying to live up to his good opinion, she was slowly discovering that she could do things that she failed at before, *be* a very different woman than she'd once been.

Because of him.

She glanced at the clock again: 6:59. Steve was due any second. The potatoes were done, her Southern fried chicken crisped to perfection, the table cozily, casually set for a quiet dinner. It didn't have to be an intimate-type dinner. Nothing "had to be" with Steve. As much time as they'd spent together, she'd sensed how carefully he avoided any further intimacies—just as she sensed the building chemistry between them. No matter how lonely, he wasn't the type to push a woman. She had absolutely no fear that anything would happen tonight, unless she wanted it to.

That thought stayed.

Leaning on the windowsill, she searched the night for a sign of his truck lights, thinking about making love with him, thinking that her feelings for him weighed on her heart like an ungiven promise.

She'd foolishly walked into so many messes with her arms wide-open. Johnny had been her worst mistake, but not the only one. There was no question she'd needed to get tougher and more realistic, if she were ever going to earn self-respect. But Steve wasn't Johnny. He'd never even tried to take advantage of her. And though she was unsure of his feelings, she knew exactly what she felt for him. Desire, longing, respect, trust, love. It was too late to deny that she was damnably, dangerously, deeply in love with that man.

She could choose to never act on those feelings. The Lord knew she was afraid of making a fool out of herself in his eyes. Maybe it was crazy to consider dancing with a wolf. But her heart knew, as sure as the beat of the pulse, that she'd never again find any man like Steve. For positive sure, Steve was the only man she'd ever known who would never let a woman down.

Nine

She was going to think he'd stood her up. Steve
glanced at the digital clock on his truck console: 10:07.
He *knew* Mary Ellen, knew damn well how she'd take
a no-show. She expected men to let her down. His
standing her up would be no surprise, not to her. She'd
slowly come to accept him as a friend, but no way, no
how, had he been able to convince that lady that she
could trust him at any other emotional level.

And being late wasn't helping his cause.

His foot ironed on the accelerator. No one else was
on the dark road. The night was windy and wild, but
the black asphalt was thankfully dry. He could push
seventy on the straightaways. It was just the curves
that bogged him down, and the whole damn road
seemed to be curves. His pulse was racing, and the
clock kept ticking.

In his mind, he saw the mental picture of an hour-glass draining sand faster than a sieve. There was more at stake than this one night. The problem of time was bigger than that. In less than two weeks he had to transport the wolf pack and the cubs, wrap this project up and move on. He needed weeks with Mary Ellen, not days. She fit in his life like a key in a lock—he was *crazy* about that woman—but getting her to believe that was tougher than uphill sledding.

Steve knew from his work that a man couldn't force trust, not with a wild animal, and never with a wounded one. His lady was as fragile as a bruised rose. He knew how she looked at him, how she was with him—hell, a forest fire could spontaneously combust from the amount of frustrated chemistry between them—but she was obviously afraid to cross that intimate line. And being late—being this *damned* late—was probably going to set his cause back a hundred years.

He hit her driveway at warp speed, braked into a fast stop and barely cut the engine before he was leaping out of the truck. Her porch light was still on—thank God she hadn't written him off completely yet—but his heart was still thundering with nerves. He hoped she was mad. She had every right to be mad. His fear, though, was that she was hurt. Too hurt to listen.

He jogged to her front step and knocked, then couldn't wait and turned the knob. Immediately he was enveloped in warmth, soft lamplight, silence. Terrifying silence. He carefully closed the door with a litany of four-letter words ramming through his mind.

One fast glance revealed how badly he'd screwed up. The card table was set up in the kitchen, with a cloth and candles worn down to nubs. He didn't need to get any closer to that gorgeous platter of fried chicken to know that it was cold, or the salad was wilted. He could smell the homemade bread. He could see the bowl of dried-up potatoes. She'd gone to all kinds of trouble. So much trouble that she'd worn herself out.

His gaze lanced, then rested softly, on her. She was curled up in the rocker, with her knees up the way she loved to sit, her eyelashes softer than spiderwebs on her cheeks. She'd dropped a magazine when she'd fallen asleep, and she was wearing a green outfit that made her look like a wood sprite. An irresistible wood sprite. Her chin was still crooked in her palm, her skin as pale as ivory under the pool of lamplight.

"Mary." He only whispered her name, yet her eyes flew open. Her smile was immediate, warm, natural. *His* smile, he'd come to think of it. There was no hint of recriminations or anger in her sleepy eyes. She should have knocked him from here to the Pacific for being so late and not calling; any other woman would have—should have—but damned if she'd ever behaved like any woman he'd ever known.

"I don't think," she murmured humorously, "that I've ever seen a mangier stray."

"Stray?" He glanced down, a little late realizing that his jacket was ripped and he was dragging mud on his boots. He'd never gotten around to brushing his hair or doing anything else about his appearance. Damn, was there no end of things going wrong for him tonight? "I didn't mean to track in. I'm sorry—"

"Life won't end if the floor gets dirty. Sit down. I was going to feed you the minute you walked in, but from the look on your face, I think I'd better pour you a drink first. Straight something. Good grief." She glanced at the clock on her way to the kitchen.

He did, too, and swallowed tar. "Mary, I wasn't late by choice."

"Of course you weren't."

"I wrecked your dinner. It looks so good. You went to a lot of trouble—" Faster than he could get a thought together, she had his hands wrapped around a shot glass filled with amber liquid. Whiskey, he guessed.

"Drink," she ordered him. "What happened to your forehead?" Her fingertips touched his brow before he could. "It looks like a granddaddy of a bruise. Are you hurt anywhere else?"

"I'm not hurt at all," he said impatiently.

"Drink," she gently ordered him again.

The whiskey gulped down like liquid fire and hit like a lightning bolt, giving him enough momentum to launch into a stumbling-fast explanation. "After I fed the pups, it was still early. But when I started hiking through the woods, I found two more traps. Fresh traps. The same type that injured White Wolf. I dismantled 'em, took them back to the truck, but I couldn't just...leave. Whoever laid them, I hoped, would come back. He'd want to check to see if he'd caught anything, and then I'd have the chance to catch him. There was no way to phone you, to tell you I'd be late. Usually I throw the cellular in the truck, but this time I left it in the trailer. Honest to Henry, I never expected to be gone for more than a couple of hours—"

"I understand. It's not a problem, Steve. With your work, I know you're not always close to a phone. Did you catch the guy?"

"No." Restlessly he rubbed the back of his neck, unsure why he felt so rattled when Mary Ellen couldn't be calmer. "I saw truck lights. Thought it might be the trapper, but it was the local law, just cruising around. Wooley Harris, you know him?"

"Sure. He's on our side."

"Yeah. I gave him the traps, told him where I found them. He said he had nothing to do, the town was quieter than a tomb, and he'd be glad to patrol the back roads and keep an eye out for the rest of the night. We'll go back there tomorrow when it's daylight, see if there are any tracks we can pin down."

"I knew there had to be something redeeming about all this Michigan spring mud. A clear tire track or footprint should be easier to find, don't you think? Do you want another drink?"

No, he didn't want another drink. He hooked her wrist in his hand, not sure why, maybe just because he needed her closer, needed to see her eyes more clearly. She didn't *seem* mad about her whole beautiful dinner ruined. She didn't seem hurt, either. She just seemed to accept that he had a darn good reason for being late and that was that. What kind of woman let a man out of hot water that easily?

Her kind, he thought. She moved past the subject of his lateness as if it never existed. "Are you hungry? I'm not sure if anything from the original menu is still salvageable, but I could throw together soup and sandwiches quicker than a blink—"

"I'm not hungry." At least not for food. She didn't pull her wrist free. He could feel the shimmer of an electric response in her pulse, but she didn't move away. No different than she'd accepted his excuses for being late, she accepted that he was a teensy bit strung out and needed taking care of. At times he'd had the uneasy feeling that she knew his moods better than he did. But not tonight. "I was afraid you'd think I stood you up," he said bluntly.

Her brows arched in surprise. "That never crossed my mind. You said you'd come. So I just assumed something held you up when you didn't get here. Did you think I wouldn't understand you had other priorities?"

There. That was what he'd expected. That velvet shine of certainty in her eyes that she wasn't his priority. His wolves were vulnerable and dependent on him; he was grateful she understood he couldn't always punch a time clock, but it wasn't just understanding about his work that he saw in those velvet eyes. It was acceptance. She never expected to be the top rung on his totem pole. Nothing he'd ever done had made the witless woman see that she was special. Alluringly, unforgettably, irresistibly special.

He yanked her wrist. Not hard. Since he'd shoot himself before hurting Mary Ellen, he'd never in a blue moon be rough with her, but the tug carried enough pressure to make her stumble toward him. Her face tilted up. He didn't know he was going to kiss her until that instant, but damned if his overloaded blood pressure didn't immediately calm down as soon as he did.

Her lips made a cushion for his awkward landing, as if she sensed the pilot was a tad short on control. When his mouth landed a second time, the awkwardness was gone. That quick, he forgot about being exhausted. He forgot about feeling wired. She tasted like sugar and softness and every wild fantasy of a lover he'd ever had. She tasted like longing and yearning.

She tasted like all the fire and desire that had been building from three seconds after he met her, and damn her, she was kissing him back as if she felt the same way.

Both surfaced for air. Not that he needed to breathe to kiss her. The annoying need for oxygen simply called for different kinds of kisses. The scrape of his tongue on the shell of her ear. The trace of his lips on her jawline, down her throat. She'd been the calm one until then. Now her hands clutched his shoulders and she was having trouble swallowing. "I guess dinner's not on your mind, huh?"

"You're on my mind."

"You came in looking so tired. You don't want to relax?" Her eyes searched his, and then wryly murmured an answer to her own question. "No. You're not in any mood to relax."

"I want to make love to you."

Telling her so bluntly lacked any claim to finesse, but it was a sure way to catch her unguarded response. He saw her breath stop, saw the fierce flash of desire in her eyes...he also saw her sudden hesitation. His lady wolf had braved the risk of dancing with him before, but he was asking for more than a dance.

Her gaze magnetized on his eyes, as if unsure what he really wanted, what making love would mean to him. He could have easily reassured her. He wanted to claim her, irrevocably and permanently. He wanted her in his bed tonight and every other night. He wanted her naked and beneath him, so hot she couldn't see straight, so wild she couldn't stand it. That was all. Nothing complicated or unclear about his motivations. Nothing tricky.

"I love you," he said.

She caught her breath again. "Steve . . . you walked in here tighter than a drum. I understand. You had one heck of an evening. You were pumped up on adrenaline—"

"I love you," he said again.

There was a five-second stretch when she might have said no, when maybe he'd have acted differently if he'd seen even the remotest trace of a "no" in her expression. He never saw no. He just saw scared.

He swooped, snaring her in his arms, taking her mouth with the volatile pressure of frustration. She didn't believe he cared. That wasn't news. And his Southern rose loved taking on things she was scared of, so her response to his cavalierly taken kiss wasn't exactly news, either. Except to his heart rate.

His heart rate was thundering louder than a jungle drumbeat. She leaned into him, her soft breasts yielding to his hard torso, her body warmer than melted sunshine. Her hands rushed up his shoulders, around his neck, as if she were starved for the touch of him. They'd danced these steps before, but this wasn't the tease and testing of the first waltzes between a man and a woman. His lady wasn't waltzing. She was flying straight into temptation with the rhythm and speed of fire. Positively she wasn't saying no.

The next time their lungs needed an oxygen break, he raveled her sweater up and over her head, then came back for another openmouthed kiss before she had a chance to shiver. Before she had the chance to think, her sweater graced the rocker arm. Seconds later, a pretty pink bra graced her lamp shade.

His neck, by then, had a familiar ache from bending down to kiss her. The difference in their heights was easily resolved when he picked her up and

wrapped her legs around his waist. He didn't need a
road map to find her bedroom. Light spilled from the
hall onto her white eyelet spread and caught the gleam
of brass bedposts. When they fell in a mutually aban-
doned heap on the mattress, the brass posts rattled and
the old bedsprings creaked. He felt a natural affinity
for that noise. His pulse was clattering and creaking,
too.

It wasn't as though his sense of honor had disappeared. It wasn't as if he didn't know that rushing her
was unfair. Maybe he was harder than quarry rock and
his blood was racing hot, but that didn't mean he
was incapable of coherent thought. Sane, rational
thoughts. Like damning her for growing up in Georgia, way too far away from him, and damning life for
throwing her curved balls that he couldn't protect her
from. She was top rung. She wasn't escaping this night
until she knew it. A man would be blessed to make her
his top priority in life. Poor baby, she was going to be
stuck learning that lesson tonight, too.

She'd have a mountain of confidence after this
night. Or he'd die trying.

He nearly died, in the battle to pull off her green
stirrup pants. The elastic waistband coiled up like a
snake and confoundedly bunched. The problem might
have been simple to resolve if he'd looked at what he
was doing. And he was looking. Just not at the elastic
waistband.

The whole bedroom was dark pewter and shadowy,
but her face was in light. The illumination spilling
from the doorway framed her throat, the splay of
mink brown hair on the white spread, her softer-than-
satin skin. He forgot the pants. Her throat needed
kissing, there, on the hot fevered pulse. Her breasts

swelled for him, the tips tightening under a merciless rain of soft, damp, evocative kisses. Her hands got in the way, trying to fumble with the buttons on his flannel shirt. And her eyes got in his way, because he kept feeling them on his face—Bambi eyes, liquid and emotive and vulnerable. His lady was coming deliciously apart for him.

And he hadn't even gotten started.

"Steve?"

She called his name on the hiss of a breath, her broken whisper making his senses swim. "I have protection," he told her, anticipating that concern before she had the chance to voice it, not wanting anything to break her mood.

"I . . . didn't have anything around," she admitted huskily.

"Sweetheart, I could have guessed that." He didn't tell her that he hated the intrusion of condoms. Nor did he mention that the mental picture of her tummy swelling with his baby stunned him with its power. He wanted to talk to her about babies. He wanted to talk to her about alternative protection methods. He wanted to talk to her about life. Just not right now.

"Steve . . . to be honest, protection wasn't exactly on my mind. At least not yet. I was just thinking that maybe you'd like to take your boots off?"

"Boots?" He was doing his damndest to be dark and dangerous, and she was thinking about *boots?*

"Don't you think you'd be a little more comfortable without your boots? And your belt. And maybe your shirt . . ."

Well, damn if there wasn't a hint of humor in those luminous eyes. Woman humor. And woman fire. He heeled off his boots, still looking in those eyes, then hustled to yank off his shirt and jeans and the rest of his clothes before that wicked-sweet invitation in her eyes disappeared. It didn't disappear. She attacked him when he still had one recalcitrant sock to deal with. He left the sock. To hell with the stupid sock. He had his hands full.

It seemed . . . it definitely seemed . . . that he didn't need to worry about her liking his body. Her fingertips danced through the coarse hair on his chest. Her palms kneaded and stroked on an uninhibited discovery mission, and she followed the trail of her hands with the trail of her lips. Her cheek nuzzled the curve of his neck. Her tongue eventually found its way to his navel.

He'd never been assaulted before, not by a woman hell-bent on cherishing him, all of him, now, immediately, as if a clock were ticking on a bomb and she might never have another chance. Her leg twisted over him, pulling him closer, pulling him to her, anchoring him as if she had the physical power to make a two-hundred-pound man do any fool thing she wanted.

Which she did. He'd have done anything for her, climb skyscrapers in a single bound, be a bird, be a plane, be any damn thing she asked him. She loved him. He'd guessed that, hoped that, believed that from a dozen clues in her behavior before this. But he didn't *know*, not for sure, until he experienced the emotion pouring from her now. Her skin glowed like moonlight in the dark room, her arms curling around him, the fierce wanting in her eyes enough to drive a man crazy.

For the first time he understood—really understood—why his wolves howled. He threw the pillows on the floor and twisted her beneath him. It took a second and a half to take care of protection—longer than eternity—and then she wrapped her legs around him with a feline husky groan. Her back arched when she felt his slow, sliding intrusion, and a shiver rippled through her whole body as he filled her. Her mouth sought his, sealed with his, in a kiss as intimate as a vow, as helpless as a secret.

He'd experienced lust before. He knew what love was. But he'd never found a woman who matched him like a soul mate, the wildness in her an incendiary flame of hunger in him—a hunger made up of her taste, her touch, the sough of her breath, the honeyed scent coming off her skin like a feminine drug that, damn, his heart was already hopelessly addicted to. She belonged. Not to him, but with him.

The bedposts clanged and the mattress creaked and squeaked. Not so fast, he kept warning himself. The ardent, urgency of her response was going straight to his head, when he knew damn well that her fears and insecurities hadn't instantly disappeared. The last thing he wanted was for Mary to feel seduced, rushed, blindsided by the speed of runaway emotions. But damn. To save his life he couldn't find the brakes on this 747. The rhythm she asked for, the rhythm she seemed to need from him, was wild and wicked and elemental. Fire raced through his bloodstream, heating his bones to liquid and making his skin slick and slippery. He watched her, protectively, possessively, watched her eyes turn dazed and smoky, watched her body bow in tension and blind need.

How could this be wrong? He ignored those warning instincts and worry was tossed out the window.

Nothing mattered but now. He'd dreamed she'd feel this way with him. Free. Free to be earthy and uninhibited. Free to be gentle. Free to be shy if she felt shy, wanton if she felt wanton, so free that she could dive straight off a cliff and trust, without doubt, that he'd be there to catch her.

She called his name, urgently, hoarsely. That ended his last claim on sanity. He took her, spinning and spiraling, straight off that cliff with him. And caught her. With all the love he had in him.

Steve had dozed off, but Mary Ellen couldn't sleep . . . and didn't want to. Parts of her body still felt tender from their wild midnight ride. It was a wondrous ache. A gossamer ache. Never mind sleep. She wanted to save the lingering feeling of intimacy and belonging for as long as she could.

His hair was rumpled, and he slept with the pillow bunched under his stubbly cheek, his long body sprawled every which way. He was a cover stealer, she'd discovered. And a stubborn man even in sleep, because when she'd tried to steal out of bed, he'd scooped her right back into his arms without ever opening his eyes.

She couldn't seem to tire of looking at him. Her mood was wondrous . . . but as fragile as a crystal snowflake. Passion wasn't new to her, but no man had ever ignited her heart the way Steve had. Johnny had considered himself a skilled lover. And he had been. But skill alone didn't compare to a man who laid himself bare and railroaded—exquisitely railroaded—his lover to be equally emotionally honest.

He'd told her he loved her. Not once, but several times. He didn't know the *real* Mary Ellen, of course, the lady with the history of making bungling, embarrassing mistakes of the heart. He didn't have the total picture, so she'd be crazy to believe those three precious words. But she believed in—as she once hadn't—her right to love and make love with him.

Her hands protectively pulled up the blanket around his shoulders, tucking out the cold spots. She'd always taken for granted that old stereotype about wolves being loners—until she met him and his animal kindred spirits. Wolves were sociable, loyal, loving, fiercely devoted to family and those they cared for. Like him. Her lover, her Steve, was never a loner by choice, only circumstance.

When he'd first walked in last night, he'd been strung out and wired tight and she'd had no idea they'd end up making love. Still, on her soul, she had no regrets. There was no man alive who believed in her the way Steve did. There was no one else who'd ever helped her change and see the possibilities about who she was as a woman...and who she could be. She loved him. To never express what he meant to her would have been wrong, no matter what the risks to her heart.

She'd never kidded herself about those risks. He was leaving soon. Rationally she knew that, just as she knew that ultimately he needed a stronger, surer woman for a mate, not someone who was always hung up on a million failings as she was. She understood that, *really* understood that, yet she found it amazing that she'd ever been afraid of anything before. She knew what real fear was now. Because she was damnably afraid her heart might never recover when he left.

She could have sworn he was still sound asleep, yet his fingertips suddenly stroked her jawline. Gently. Tenderly. "Can't sleep?"

"I'm fine." One of the dozens of fibs she'd told him, she thought ruefully, but the truth was so hard to say. She didn't want to sleep. She didn't want this night to end. She wanted that bond between them to make an indelible memory, a secret she could always have and hold.

He shifted, scrunching his pillow under her head so they shared the same space. Even in the charcoal darkness, she could feel his eyes on her face. Wolf eyes. Boundless, deep, mirror-to-the-soul eyes, resting on her face like the physical brush of a caress. "You're a wonder, Mary Barnett," he murmured. "I'm not sure I understand what you do to me. I don't have to understand. You're a treasure I never expected to find."

"No treasure," she said. "Just a plain old ordinary woman."

"That's how much you know. Plain old ordinary women don't turn a man's head to mush and cinders. I'm wasted, lady. You did that. In fact, I'm holding you entirely responsible for my completely losing control."

She chuckled softly at his teasing. His voice was velvet with sleep, seductive and male, the glow from his praise spreading through her whole body. "I think both of us lost a little control."

"A little?"

"Okay. We both lost the whole kit and kaboodle." The fierce warmth in his eyes made her feel impossibly shy. She groped for something less volatile to talk about. "If you're awake... I was worried that you'd wake up hungry. You completely missed dinner."

"Dinner sounds good. I have to admit, I'm starved."

Of course he was. Concern immediately sent her mind spinning. "The sponge cake'll still be edible. Maybe a little dry. I'm not sure what else I can salvage from the original dinner, but there have to be things I could rustle up—"

"Mary?"

"Hmm?"

"The sponge cake sounds good. But I'm not hungry for sponge cake."

"A sandwich?"

"Not a sandwich, either. I'm starving. Honestly starving. But there's only one taste I really have a craving for—"

"What?" She lifted her hand to push back the covers, prepared to leap out of bed and fix a feast.

He pounced before she had the chance. His mouth took hers, silkier and softer than a spring wind, then deeper, harder, wilder. The feast he had in mind, she discovered quickly, was her.

Ten

Watching her fly around the kitchen, Steve wasn't sure whether he wanted to strangle her or kiss her. Unfortunately, both options required body contact. She was moving too fast for him to try either.

"You'd better like French toast," Mary Ellen warned him. "I made enough for the marines."

"French toast'd be just great."

She set his plate down with a grin. "Pretty easy to please a man who hasn't had a meal since noon yesterday. I suspect you'd go for a piece of cardboard right about now."

"Well, this isn't cardboard. And it really looks delicious." It did. She made French toast the real-life French way, with crusty bread, slightly dried and crisped to a delectable cinnamon brown. He'd have dived in any other time. He'd never been prone to anxiety attacks in a crisis, but from the acid swirling in his stomach, he was having one now. He wasn't positive if he was capable of swallowing.

Carrying a yellow ceramic pot, Mary Ellen brought napkins and syrup to the table. It was still early. Barely seven, and still musty dark outside. Steve had hoped she'd sleep in—he knew intimately, unforgettably why she needed more rest—but she'd bolted out of the bed the instant she heard the shower running. When he came out, she was already cooking breakfast, wearing a thick rose robe, her face freshly scrubbed and her hair tucked behind her ears. Her cheek still had a pillow crease. She looked edible. Edible, huggable, holdable and lovable... but no way was she getting close enough for him to do any of those things.

There was a distance in her eyes this morning. A Grand Canyon chasm of a distance, and guilt pricked his conscience like porcupine quills, because he knew damn well he'd caused it.

Never mind how willing his Southern rose had been last night. Seducing her had been a mistake. In the heat of the moment, she'd definitely seemed to like being rushed, swept away, but dammit, he knew Mary Ellen Barnett. Throw her to the wolves and she thrived—but she never anticipated that ahead of time. The lady he loved only gained confidence one way, the hard way, by confronting whatever she was afraid of and seeing the results for herself. Seducing her stole those kinds of choices. If he'd waited for her to come to him, he would have *known* how she felt. And so would she.

Her fork hovered midair. "You don't like my French toast?"

Tarnation. Things were shaky enough without risking hurting her feelings, too. "Are you kidding?

It's delicalucious, as my dad used to say.'' He shoveled in a mouthful and started praying fast that it would go down.

"How was White Wolf yesterday?''

"Still limping, but better. Truthfully, once I knew he wasn't suffering from any broken bones, I was more worried about how the others would treat him than the injury itself. There was always a chance the pack members would have turned on him.''

"You never told me that. You mean they would have attacked him? When he was injured?''

"They would have attacked him *because* he was injured. Now don't look like that, sweet pea. It's just nature, the order of their world. Wolves traditionally help each other, but their leader is a logical exception to that rule. If they sense their boss is weak, no longer capable, they put another in his place. It's their way of surviving.''

"Well, I don't like it.''

"Didn't think you would, Ms. Softie. But since nothing happened, there's no reason to worry. Maybe the pack intuited that this is a recoverable injury. Whatever, they're still accepting him as King Pin.'' Steve wanted to believe it was a good sign they were talking so easily. Only he'd never bought swampland in Arizona. This was a first-time morning after. Where were the nerves? Where was the awkwardness? As if they were good old pals, Mary affectionately squeezed his shoulder when she brought him another glass of orange juice.

Nothing he needed to worry about, she seemed to be telling him. We slept together, no big deal. Only he'd hoped that making love *was* a big deal. He'd hoped to deal with a mountain of nerves and awkwardness and insecurities this morning. All he was getting was smiles.

Those comfortable, natural smiles were damn near enough to terrify a man.

"I know how much the pups have grown. You're about ready to move them, aren't you? Have you set a specific date?"

There, he thought with relief. Finally an opening. A chance to bring their future into the picture. "Yeah. I've been thinking about a week from tomorrow. Wednesday. I'll fly them over to their old stomping ground on the island by seaplane, probably stay there a week, just to make sure they settle in okay. And after that... Yellowstone. Have you ever been to Yellowstone?"

She shook her head.

"I think you'd love it," he said carefully. "There are wild parts of the park, some so beautiful they'd take your breath away. I swear it's God's country."

"Sounds gorgeous."

He saw honest interest in her expression. He saw curiosity. But a blowtorch couldn't seem to melt that distance in her eyes, as if hearing about his goals and plans was wonderful, but totally remote from her. He tried again. "In that part of the country, there are lots of small towns. Lots of places where a fix-it lady could find work to do. I really think you would love it there."

"I'd love to see it." The instant she saw his plate was empty, she swiftly got up and shifted dishes to the counter. "What time are you meeting with Wooley Harris about that trapper this morning?"

"Around ten. It was about the earliest we could connect. He knew I had to get breakfast to the pups before doing anything else.'' The acid in his stomach was churning double-time. He'd never resented his wolves before, never resented any of the responsibilities that came with his work, but he just didn't want to leave her. If he had any choice at all, they'd be back in her bed, making that old mattress squeak in stereo. They'd had no problems with distance last night. They'd had no problems at all.

"Good heavens, I just noticed the time. You really have to get going then, don't you?"

"I should," he admitted unwillingly. He'd seen the blasted clock, too. Just as fast as she'd hustled those plates, now she hustled to fetch his jacket. She couldn't wait to get rid of him, he thought glumly. Despair had never felt this terrifying.

"Steve . . . you'll be careful, won't you? I don't like anything about this trapper business. And I keep thinking this guy could easily have a gun—''

"I'm not about to do anything foolhardy. You know me better than that, and this won't be the first time I've had to handle a problem like this.''

"I know you can handle yourself.'' She lifted his jacket so he could stick his arms in. When he turned around, she found a speck of lint on his shoulder to brush off. "But I just want you to be extra careful. You didn't get a lot of sleep last night, and you must be tired—''

"The best tired I can remember," he said quietly. "I wouldn't have slept at all, if I could have helped it.''

A soft glow flushed her cheeks, and for an instant he caught the shine of emotion in her eyes. A naked, intimate shine, just for him. But then she quickly dropped her gaze. "Steve . . .'' She chuckled suddenly, and found another piece of lint on his jacket sleeve to fleck off. "I can't seem to stop thinking about this real embarrassing story. Do you remember the first person you fell for?"

The only woman he'd fallen for—who made any difference—was her. But he said "Sure" so she'd tell him whatever was on her mind.

"Well I can, too. In fact, I can remember like it was yesterday, the first time I was in love. Deeply, irrevocably in love. We were going to be married, have kids, live happily ever after. Neither heaven nor earth was going to tear us apart. I was sixteen at the time, you understand. And I decided all this on our first date." Her tone was a sassy Southern drawl, light and breezy, inviting him to share the humor. "The boy—he had a ten-buck bet with the guys on how far he could get in the back seat of his daddy's Buick. Naturally it never crossed my mind that he wasn't as deeply, irrevocably in love as I was."

She paused. That was the punch line, apparently when he was supposed to laugh and agree that she'd been damn stupid and naive. Steve was more inclined to find that boy in Georgia and smash his face in, but he reined back that prehistorical response. This was clearly quicksand for Mary. She'd told him a few of her youthful escapades before, always assuming that he'd see the humor when all he'd ever seen was how an open and vulnerable heart had been badly hurt. And she had no reason to bring up that story—not right after they'd made love—unless it meant something to her. "You think," he asked gently, "that I would take advantage of you like that?"

"No." Her eyes shot to his. "Heavens, *no!*" She gestured. "I was just trying to tell you that when I was younger, I used to misread people's feelings all the time. I had a bad habit of building fairy castles out of sand. Thank heavens I grew up. You don't have to worry that I misread anything into last night that you didn't intend."

"Mary...I *love* you."

She smiled. "I love you, too." She raised up on tip-toe and kissed him. A kiss she'd give a brother or a best friend. There was love, and there was love. She wasn't holding him accountable for anything he'd said in the heat of passion.

Frustration coiled inside him. Frustration—and fear. He *wanted* her to hold him accountable for those words of love. He wanted her to see what they had together, what they *were* together.

He respected that Mary Ellen needed more time to know him if she were ever to have confidence in her feelings. But he was running out of time. Fast. In less than two weeks, he had to be gone. And unless he found some way to convince her that what they had was infinitely precious, he was damned scared he was going to lose her.

She'd handled that perfectly, she thought. So perfectly that even days later she could still replay that whole morning-after conversation in her mind and feel good about it. Thankfully she hadn't done anything stupid—like throwing herself into his arms and admitting he meant the world to her. And she hadn't done anything embarrassing—like cry—even when he talked about leaving for Yellowstone.

His time in the U.P. was finite. She'd always known that. Just as there was an end point to the pups' dependence on Steve, there had to be an end point to her dependence on him, too. She'd grown, loving him.

She'd grown and changed and discovered love, real love, and no way was she going to regret an instant of the time she'd spent with him.

"Stick close, okay?"

"Honestly, Rawlings. I couldn't be any closer without a leash around my wrist."

"A leash?" He scratched his chin. "I like that idea."

"You would. I swear you were born in the wrong time. You'd fit right in with the cavemen and all those other guys with protective ideas about women."

"Listen, Ms. Sass, that trapper is still running around loose. And I just don't think it's a good idea for you to be wandering around the woods until we know who that jerk is."

When she feigned a huge yawn of boredom, he cuffed her neck with an exasperated chuckle. He'd wanted her to stay home, she knew. But it was Sunday night; she didn't have to be at Samson's, and although she had half-finished fix-it jobs cluttering her living room, everything would wait. She'd kept her mood light for Steve, but the ache in her heart was becoming a pervasive flu—she wasn't going to have many more chances to be with him . . . or to see the mangy, monster pups she'd come to love.

Heavy dust gray clouds were scuttling across the sky. Sunset was still an hour away, but the evening was already broody and chill and threatening rain. She perched on a rock and unscrewed the thermos lid, pouring a quick mug of coffee, while Steve hiked the last few feet to the den.

Her participation wasn't required—or desired. She understood that minimal human contact was best for the pups; she just wanted to watch. And did, as the minimonsters picked up Steve's scent and poured through the ledge opening with frisky, stumbling enthusiasm.

Her gaze softened helplessly. They'd grown so much. Their ears were perky now. They could growl and howl just like the big guys. And White Wolf's son, the pure-white baby who looked like his clone, had already established himself as Mr. Alpha Male, even if he did still fall over his own feet half the time.

She pulled off her gloves and wrapped her hands around the thermos mug, her eyes homing in on Steve. He was hunkered down, the wind riffling through his hair, surrounded by the yipping, noisy pups. At this point, Hamlet and Thunder and Scarlett regularly brought the young ones choice tidbits from the wild, so Steve no longer really needed to feed them. But the urchins had had a rough start, so he was adding vitamin supplements—in the form of treats—for as long as he could.

She heard a sound behind her, and turned her head to see White Wolf only a few yards away. "Hi there, sweetie," she whispered. "You coming to see me?"

Apparently so, because the big wolf limped closer, his tail high, his soul-deep eyes on her face, looking terrifying and feral and strong enough to tear her apart in a blink. He pranced the last few steps to her side, then lifted his snout and nudged off her stocking cap.

"Hey!" she protested, but she didn't mean it. The wolf backed off a few steps, but he cocked his head and swished his silver-white tail, as if inviting her to play.

"You want my hat, big guy?" She picked up the cap and tossed it. He bounded after it, then, unfortunately, took off with his new treasure. When he loped back from behind a stand of pines, her cap was gone, but he cocked his head and swished his tail as if inviting her to give him something else. "Forget it, doofus, that's the last item of clothing you get from me. How about if we just play with a stick?"

She picked up a twig but was careful to toss it low, understanding that he might interpret a raised stick in her hand as an aggressive gesture. He pounced on the twig and tossed it a few times, then sashayed back to her. His willingness to play warmed her heart. They'd come so far. Just like Steve, the white wolf was playful and full of mischief and affectionate...and lonely. Lonely enough to accept her human company, even if she wasn't normally his cup of tea.

She hurled the stick again for him, but the game, on the spin of a second, was over. White Wolf suddenly growled, low and sharply. His teeth bared and his ruff fur stood up. Mary Ellen frowned, unsure if she'd done something to upset him.

He pivoted around, pawing the ground, sniffing, then snarling again. High on the ridge, beyond the pines, she heard the sound of a branch snapping. White Wolf immediately plunged through the woods in that direction. Worried about his injury—no matter how well he was playing and moving around, the wolf was still hampered by that limp—Mary Ellen took off after him. All she wanted to do was keep him in sight, so she could call Steve, tell him if White Wolf was getting into trouble.

She clawed her way up the ridge, and reached the top breathless. The other wolves had disappeared from sight, which was hardly surprising—none of them came closer to her the way White Wolf did. She saw a shadow streak behind the branches of a massive blue spruce. White Wolf. But beyond, just beyond, she caught movement and color. A man, wearing army fatigue colors, and the shine of something metal that he dropped while he was running.

"Steve!" Fear barreled through her veins. Fear that the man had a gun and would shoot White Wolf, fear that the wolf would attack the man, and most of all, the dread-pounding anxiety that something or someone was going to get hurt unless something happened, now, fast, immediately. She yelled for Steve again, sure he could hear her. He wasn't that far away. And being a true-blue coward—a skilled and accomplished coward—she intended to take a fast powder out of harm's way, out of Steve's way, out of everyone's way. In that instant when she turned, though, she recognized that clump of metal in the muddy ground.

It was a trap. The capsule picture shot through her mind of White Wolf lying in that bloody mess, his paw clamped in a disgustingly cruel trap identical to this one. Her eyes flew up. The crashing sounds in the woods were coming closer instead of getting farther. The intruder had switched back—the idiot must have finally realized that his best chance of reaching safety was heading for the road and his vehicle. But the effect of his changing directions meant that he was suddenly thrashing through the brush less than thirty feet from her. And damn. White Wolf was stalking him in a blur of white misty fur in and out of the tree shadows.

She ran. The Lord knew she'd done some stupid, impulsive things in her time, but this one just didn't seem to be a choice. She could smell a disaster in the making, feel it in the panicked slam of her heartbeat.

The wolf was going to attack the jerk; there'd be hell to pay if that happened, for Steve, for White Wolf, for all the wolves.

The man galloped through the woods yards from her, then mere feet. He was going to pass right by her. She didn't stop to think. She had no *time* to think. There was only going to be one chance to do anything. She leapt on his back like a tick on a hound, screaming, *"Steve!"* and *"No,* White Wolf!"

A flash of manic humor struck her at that instant—only a damn fool would expect a wild wolf to obey or give a royal hoot about a human command. That news flash was a tad irrelevant. Oh God, was she in trouble. The force of her leap didn't knock him down, but the man swore like a marine in the shock of surprise. He tried to buck her off, swearing, yelling, his hands trying to claw at her legs.

He didn't appreciate the monkey on his back. She was scared to death she was going to be hurt and hurt good. An unwashed smell reeked off the man.

The muscles in her legs cramped from trying so hard to hold on, and with a sense of despair, she knew there was no way, no how, she had the physical strength bring him down. He had a gun, a rifle, which she didn't realize until it clattered to the ground in the fracas. At least temporarily that gun wasn't a threat to her or White Wolf, but he thrashed around, trying to dislodge her. Her head smacked against a hardwood tree trunk. She saw stars. She saw herself, starring in a Laurel and Hardy embarrassing comedy about a foolish woman riding a human bucking bronco, holding on not out of any bravery or courage but because she just plain didn't know what else to do.

"Schneider."

Steve's voice filtered through the chaos of noise and confusion. Until then, she hadn't had the functioning brain to recognize the trapper as Richard Schneider from the bar, but she recognized her lover's voice just fine. On New Year's Eve in Times Square, she'd know that velvet, slow, lazy voice of his. Steve could probably defuse bombs with that certain tone. God knew, he could make a woman lose her heart. Schneider may not know how much trouble he was in, but she sure did.

"Schneider. I want you to turn around, slow, and let her down real, real carefully. You don't want to risk her getting hurt. Trust me, I will not be a happy camper if I find one bruise on her because of you. That's it. Just move real slow and easy and everything's gonna be fine...."

Some parties dragged on forever. By the time Mary Ellen was curled up in the corner of Steve's couch in the trailer, the night was pitch-black. She'd barely collapsed before he handed her a shot glass of Southern bourbon. She hated bourbon. The pups were fine. White Wolf was fine. Everybody was fine—except for Richy Schneider, who hadn't been real happy when Wooley Harris found a pouch of marijuana in his pocket, not to mention the nice fat charge wrapped around his neck for illegal trapping. But the excitement was finally over, and she'd be doing fine, too, except that when she swallowed a rancid gulp of that bourbon, Steve shoved another shot glass in front of her.

"I'd rather have poison," she informed him.

"Cater to me, okay? My hands are still shaking. It'd help me a lot if you took a drink."

His hands weren't shaking. Hers were. He dropped a blanket over her shoulders, big enough to swallow her twice over. She was having the hardest time meeting his eyes. "I really feel ... stupid," she admitted.

"Stupid?" Steve's eyebrows arched in surprise. "I'll strangle you if you ever do anything that dangerous again, but the only reason we nailed the bastard was because of you. Why on earth would you feel stupid?"

"Because..." She gestured with a hand, feeling awkward and frustrated at even trying to explain. "Jumping on his back was an idiotic thing to do. I didn't *think*. He was too big, nobody I could possibly handle. But I just had no way to *do* anything."

"Mary, what the Sam Hill did you expect of yourself?" Steve shook his head. "So you reacted without thinking and you scared me half to death. But I swear you have more courage than anyone I've ever met—courage at the instinct level, the heart level. Can't you be proud of what you did?"

The image of her flying around Schneider's back like a monkey was more cringe material than the stuff of pride. But his praise, the heat and intensity in his voice, warmed her. She met his eyes. As if a light bulb switched on in her mind, shining softly, gaining power, she suddenly saw herself as he did.

He loved her. The emotion was in his eyes, in his smile. She knew he cared, but love—she'd been so sure he didn't know the *real* Mary Ellen well enough to love her. In wanting his respect, she'd worked so hard to hide her flaws and secrets. She'd hidden the whole mortifying story of Johnny. Yet Steve had caught her a dozen times doing impulsive things now, like that monkey scene in the woods, and he persisted in finding courage in her character.

Giving herself credit came hard, but Steve's stubbornness made her realize that there *had* been courage involved. Guts, of a brand she'd never had growing up. Standing up for herself had always been tough, and maybe it always would be. But for the first time, she recognized that Steve wasn't seeing her through rose-colored glasses. She really was a different woman than she used to be. And the way he looked at her, there was suddenly no chance of stopping the drip and sizzle of hope from gaining hold in her heart.

"I'm cold," she admitted suddenly.

"You want me to get you another blanket?"

She shook her head. "I don't want another blanket. And for sure, I don't want any more bourbon."

"Well, then, I'll..." He picked up on her sudden, slow smile. "Maybe," he said, "you'd better spend the night here."

"Maybe I'd better."

"Maybe you'd better spend the night in my bed."

"I think I should."

"With me."

"I don't think there's any chance I could warm up any other way," she said primly, so primly that he laughed out loud. And then scooped her off the couch and took off with her.

"You always going to sass me this way, Barnett? Jump off cliffs, scare me half to death and then turn me inside out with your sass?"

"Always," she agreed. And locked in his strong arms, she kissed him. The sound of that word "always" drummed in her ears, echoed like the promise of thunder that brought spring rain. She tested it in her heart's ear and thought...maybe.

Maybe...she could make that word "always" a reality.

Maybe, just maybe...she was strong enough to hold this man, her lover, the lone wolf of her heart.

So far, for once in her life, she hadn't done anything to screw up. For once in her life—just once—she begged the Fates for some luck on her side. Her heart was wrapped in a fragile noose. She wasn't about to forget how little time left she had with Steve.

Eleven

Mary Ellen was testing the motor on a recalcitrant router when she heard the knock on the door. It couldn't be Steve—he'd just dropped her home less than an hour ago, because both of them had a Monday morning filled with chores. Expecting a potential customer, she wiped her hands on a rag and jogged for the door.

The instant she turned the knob, she saw the roses. Two dozen, long stemmed. Odd, when roses were such a universal feminine favorite, how the look of them caused an immediate sick thud in her pulse.

Her gaze traveled up and froze on the familiar face: the boyish grin, the sweep of blond hair, the elegant bones, the laugh lines around his eyes. Johnny hadn't changed an ounce in the past few months. The sick-thick feeling in her throat made her voice sound as if it were coming from a million miles away. "Johnny! What are you doing here?"

He responded with a cocky chuckle. "Surprised to see me, huh? Let me tell you, it was no small job tracking you down to this Podunker town."

"Why on earth did you come?"

"Can't you guess? I came to find you. Are you gonna let me in?"

She let him in, fast, and closed the door even faster. Even though she wasn't expecting Steve, she was slammingly conscious that she'd never told him about Johnny or about being jilted...but one look at her ex-fiancé, and the memories came flooding back. The years of thinking of herself as a problem that needed fixing; the humiliating memory of standing alone at the altar, painfully aware that she'd half expected this to happen, because everything she'd ever done had turned out just as disastrously.

Last night she'd made love with Steve as if "always" were a promise on the table. Now the hope of that "always" took a sudden harsh emotional nose-dive.

"What do you want?" she asked Johnny.

"You sound real cold. And I guess I deserve that. I owe you an apology about the wedding and all. I admit it, Mary Ellen, I got cold feet. But I've had a lot of time to do some serious thinking. The whole family helped knock some sense into me."

"I imagine they did," she said dryly. Johnny's clan had never accepted her with open arms, but they were old-line Southern money and old-line respectability. They wouldn't like one of theirs to draw public attention by jilting a bride.

He tried out his most charming smile. "I want you back, sweetheart. I know I made a mistake. I know you probably need some time to forgive me. But we had something really good going, I realize that now, and I'll do whatever I have to to win you back."

She hesitated. Lord, just once she wanted to handle an awkward situation well. Hadn't she grown? Hadn't she changed? Hadn't she *believed* she wasn't the blundering klutz she used to be? "Johnny, I'm sorry you traveled all this way, if that was your only purpose in coming. I wish you'd called first. I could have told you how I felt—"

He interrupted her midstream by draping the roses in her arms. "Here, honey."

The gesture was just like him. "The roses are beautiful. Thank you." She took a breath. "But I don't want them, Johnny. I'm sorry, but any feelings I had for you are long gone."

"You're still angry."

"No."

"I hurt you. I understand, and I'm sorry. *Really* sorry."

"I'm not hurt," she said quietly, "not anymore. To be honest, I'm grateful that you got those cold feet, because it made me realize a relationship would never have worked for us."

"You *couldn't* have forgotten what wonderful times we had."

She pricked her wrist on a thorn, thinking that he was right. They'd had some wonderful times together. No one could be more fun than Johnny. He'd been a salve to the chronic sore she had about feeling low about herself, so she'd been hungry to believe in those good times, hungry to believe they really meant something. "We played well together. We'd never have lived well together. We're not alike in any way that matters. We don't value any of the same things—"

"Yeah, we do," he said confidently, "and I'm more than willing to prove it to you."

Alarm shot through her pulse when he started to take off his coat. "You can put that right back on. You're not staying."

"Oh, yeah, I am. I got a look at this shacky town on the drive in. You don't belong here. You belong with me. And I'm staying until I convince you to come back to me."

Samson watched her peel off her jacket and reach for the bar apron. "I hear you got a boyfriend back in town."

She whirled around. "Oh, God. He isn't here, is he?"

"Not now. Came by earlier, looking for you, stuck around for a little chitchat."

"Steve wasn't here, was he?"

"Nope. Ain't seen Steve all day."

Neither had Mary Ellen, but they were bound to connect soon. She filched a packet of antacids from her purse and popped two. They weren't working. The dread-sick feeling in her stomach had persisted all day. She'd tried being tactful with Johnny. She'd tried being nice. She'd even tried the renegade outlandish idea of being honest. All she'd won was an awkward pass— and Johnny's repeat promise that he wasn't going anywhere.

Lord, if she'd ever accumulated any brownie points Upstairs, she needed to cash them in now. Before coming to work, she'd stopped for gas and at the grocer's—and almost had a stroke. Maybe she'd managed to throw him out of her place that morning, but the blasted man had had a busy afternoon, talking to people all over town, telling him that he was her fiancé. Samson, like everyone else, seemed charmed by Johnny's romantic plight. She understood. She'd been charmed by his effusive romantic ways, too—once.

Romantic gestures were wonderful, but only if there was love behind them. All it took to buy roses was money, nothing hard for a man with pockets full of that green stuff. A man who crawled through the mud to put a soft-eyed cub in her arms... Now *that* was romantic. A man who stood by her dreams and goals, no matter how unlike his own—now *there* were the guts of real love. A man who made her come apart with his touch, with his look, with the emotion in his eyes... *that* was what mattered to her.

But Steve. Lord, what was he going to think if he found out about Johnny? That she was a dimwit who fell for a charmer? That she was so shallow she couldn't recognize a manipulative boy from a real man?

She heard voices coming from the bar, customers were waiting, and hurriedly she pushed through the swinging doors, but her stomach still felt queasy. It had been sheer blind luck that Steve was busy getting the wolves ready to move to the island, or he would undoubtedly have heard about Johnny already.

Not long ago, she'd sworn that her days of causing awkward, embarrassing scenes were behind her. She'd finally developed some poise and self-assurance. She'd turned into a woman that Steve was proud to have on his arm. Dammit, she'd turned into a woman *she* was proud to be.

But no way could she stand back and allow her addlepated ex-fiancé to threaten everything that mattered to her. It was past time she told Steve about Johnny. She no longer wanted to keep secrets—any secrets—from the man she loved, but in the meantime, this wasn't his problem. It was hers.

Rats.

Sometimes a woman had to do what a woman had to do.

Wooley Harris lifted the old metal coffeepot with a grimace of apology. "Might be a last cup left in here, but afraid it's going to taste like dregs."

"I don't mind." Steve accepted the chipped coffee mug and stretched back in the wooden office chair. Between taking care of the wolves and making arrangements to move the animals to the island, he'd been running all day. He was beat. All he wanted to do was see Mary—all day, he'd been in a hurry to see Mary—but for another hour he knew darn well she was busy with the dinner crowd.

The county building was just a hop-skip across the road to the bar, and when Wooley invited him to shoot the breeze for a few minutes, Steve hadn't argued. The coffee gave him a chance to refuel and gather his patience. He was coiled tighter than a spring. Wooley was bored—too little crime to keep him busy, he claimed—and the older man was distractingly good company. The conversation wandered from town news to politics, then predictably turned into a rehash of the situation with Richy Schneider.

"I knew he was using," Wooley said, "I just never caught anything on him before. Mix drugs and a real macho complex, and you always got trouble. I'm just real sorry he picked your wolves to prey on.''

"At least he was caught before there was any more harm done. Hard to fight that kind of enemy. Good people have honest concerns about wolves in their backyard. Give everyone a chance to talk and learn from each other, and a middle ground isn't that hard to find. But jerks like Schneider muck up the real issues for both sides...." At the sudden sound of screeching brakes outside, Steve abruptly turned his head toward the window.

"What's going on?" Wooley heard the sound, too, and swung out of his chair.

Steve reached the window first. "Looks like there's some kind of commotion going on in front of Samson's." The truck driver who'd screeched his brakes was already moving on. Once the truck passed, Steve could see the crowd spilling out in the street by the bar entrance. A tall blond man suddenly backed out of Samson's, his arms raised in a protective gesture. Steve's gaze narrowed sharply on the stranger.

"I know who that is," Wooley muttered. "Have you...uh...heard about..."

"Yeah, I heard about him," Steve said mildly. "Couldn't go anywhere today, in town or out, without someone making a point of telling me he was here."

"That figures, knowing how this town loves to spread gossip...well, hell. I don't believe this. What exactly is that woman of yours *doing?*"

Steve had already noted the crowd scattering toward Mary Ellen's rather exuberant exit from the bar. "Offhand," he murmured, "I'd say she was attempting to threaten the gentleman's life with a chair."

Wooley shot him a sidelong glance, and then they both bolted for their jackets and peeled outside. Undoubtedly the little scene wouldn't have drawn so much attention if the whole town hadn't been winter-bored and dying for a little excitement. Thankfully Steve was a head taller than most. Otherwise he'd have a hard time seeing over the bodies and commotion.

His pulse was beating like a manic clock. All day he'd heard about Johnny, heard about how the guy was trying to woo her back. Mary had always avoided the subject of her ex-fiancé with the skill of an escape artist. He'd long suspected that the jerk was responsible for delivering a wounding blow to her self-confidence, and he'd almost been glad when the guy showed up. It was a way for Mary Ellen to dot her *i*'s on unfinished business, to be sure how she felt. About him, about them, about whatever affected their past.

Not *too* glad, though. One look, and Steve could see the guy was a looker. As handsome as a woman's dream, tall but not *too* tall, with the clothes and cars and looks that advertised financial security and a stable life-style—the kinds of things Steve could never promise her.

The argument was heating up, loud enough for him to catch the words now, and again his muscles tensed with strain. It took every ounce of self-control he'd ever had—or prayed for—to stand still and do nothing. The lady he loved had a mountain of pride about coping on her own. Steve knew better than to interfere. He'd almost lost her once, assuming she wanted him to leap in and take over for her. It was a mistake he'd sworn to never make again, and he knew how much was at stake. He knew, but, *damn,* if staying out of this wasn't the hardest thing he'd ever done. There were times when a lady needed a hero. He wanted to be one for her. He wanted to leap in and pulverize that pretty boy's face.

"What the heck are you *doing?*" Johnny yelled at her. "Quit poking that chair at me!"

"The devil I will. I told you *no* every which way I know how, Johnny. And you heard me. You just didn't want to listen. Have I finally got your attention now?"

"Will you cut it out? You're gonna hurt somebody with that thing! Just put the chair down and we'll talk. You don't mean any of this."

"Hells bells. I can't believe I'm still failing to communicate." She aimed for his chest with the chair legs. "You've got two choices, dearie dumps. Either leave me alone and get out of town, or watch me smash this over your head."

"For God's sakes—"

"Get in that pretty white car of yours, Johnny."

"Mary Ellen—"

"*Now.* Get in, start that stupid thing and head straight down Main Street. I don't want to see you again. Am I finally making myself clear?" Awkwardly she hefted the chair above her head as if she meant to throw it at him. Johnny froze. Then abruptly spun around and ran.

Steve bent to Wooley and murmured under his breath, "That's my girl."

Oh, Lord. Oh, Lord. She was shaking so hard she could hardly catch her breath—and didn't even try until she saw the white tail of Johnny's car round the corner. Johnny was gone. Finally. And surely for good this time, but abruptly she realized that the bar had emptied out. Faces were in every lit window. People were everywhere. The whole darn town had witnessed the entire mortifying scene.

Then—as if she weren't already living out her worst nightmare—she spotted Steve.

Her heart sank to her shoes. He was leaning against the county building, standing next to Wooley Harris, his alpaca jacket open in the wind, one lazy boot cocked forward. No prayer was going to help her. It was obvious he'd seen the whole thing.

The instant their eyes met, he straightened and started walking toward her. There was no root cellar nearby, no handy cave, no Good Witch of the East to help her handily disappear. Every pair of eyes in town watched him cross the street, but somehow, crazily, it was as if they were suddenly alone. His gaze held her as relentlessly and inescapably as a pair of handcuffs.

The sun had just set. Rooftops were bathed in that hazy soft light. A dog was barking somewhere. Everything looked so normal; there was nothing to portend a disaster in the making. He stomped right up to her, and before she could say a word, before she could even remember how to make her vocal chords function, he swooped.

"I'm so proud of you," he whispered huskily, "that I just about can't stand it."

If that wasn't a dizzying enough thing to say, the bewildering man kissed her. Lifted her clear off her feet and claimed a deep kiss. A wild, wicked, slow kiss, as if he were crazy about her. As if they were alone in the privacy of a bedroom, and he couldn't keep his hands off her. As if her soft mouth was a connection straight to his soul.

Heaven knew, that kiss was a connection to hers. When he lifted his head, she only had a second to gulp, "Steve, that was the guy I was once engaged to."

"I figured that out, honey."

She fumbled to explain the rest. "I never meant to cause a public scene. You have to believe me. But I'd tried being nice. I'd tried being firm. I'd tried everything else I knew how to get rid of him—"

"I understand." His fingers feathered through her hair. "It's tough when you have to do tough things. Things that are especially hard for you. Everybody would get out of those kinds of awkward situations if they could, but sometimes, hell, we're all stuck with a confrontation. And I'll tell you this. I need you in my corner, Mary Ellen Barnett."

"You do?"

"I do—permanently," he affirmed. "I've never met a more strong or self-reliant woman, Ms. Barnett. You might not need a hero in your life... but I do. There are wolves at my door all the time. I need a strong, gutsy lady who's willing to protect me. You think you might consider auditioning for the job?"

She almost smiled at his gentle joke about her protecting *him*. Only there was no humor in his expression. She'd seen the look of love in his eyes before, but never like now. His voice was husky, his blue eyes intense, dark, vulnerable.

Her lone wolf, she'd long realized, was always going to be more vulnerable than other men. But she never meant him to be afraid of losing her. She touched his cheek with tenderness, with wonder. "Are you trying to say you picked me from the pack, Rawlings?"

"I'm trying to tell you there'll be no other women for me, love, not in this lifetime."

Her heart stopped, then filled to overflowing with emotion. It had taken her so long—almost too long—to understand that his need to love and be loved was as great as her own.

"There was a time," she whispered, "when I'd have been afraid to say yes. I just didn't think I was the right answer for you. But you have such a bad habit of volunteering for trouble, Steve. I swear you'd dive straight off a cliff for the things you believe in. Maybe I'd better take you on. I sure can't trust anyone else to keep you safe."

"What is this *maybe* business?"

He wasn't smiling yet, but she saw the hint of one, and that horrible vulnerability was disappearing from his eyes. She hooked her arms around his neck. "We're in public. I was trying not to embarrass you by shouting at the top of my lungs that I love you more than my life."

There was his smile. The rich, loving, private smile that he reserved just for her. He nuzzled her forehead. "I couldn't care less about the crowd, but I have to admit. I'd love to hear you shout those words when we're alone."

"So what are we doing still standing here?" she whispered. "Take me home."

*   *   *   *   *

COMING NEXT MONTH

MILLION DOLLAR SWEEPSTAKES (III)

JINGLE BELLS, WEDDING BELLS:
Silhouette's Christmas Collection for 1994

Christmas Wish List

*To beat the crowds at the malls and get the perfect present for *everyone,* even that snoopy Mrs. Smith next door!

*To get through the holiday parties without running my panty hose.

*To bake cookies, decorate the house and serve the perfect Christmas dinner—just like the women in all those magazines.

*To sit down, curl up and read my Silhouette Christmas stories!

Join *New York Times* bestselling author Nora Roberts, along with popular writers Barbara Boswell, Myrna Temte and Elizabeth August, as we celebrate the joys of Christmas—and the magic of marriage—with

JINGLE
BELLS,
WEDDING
BELLS

Silhouette's Christmas Collection for 1994.

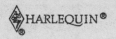 HARLEQUIN®   SUNDAYS ON CBS HARLEQUIN MOVIES WATCH FOR THEM!  Silhouette®

The movie event of the season can be the reading event of the year!

Lights... The lights go on in October when CBS presents Harlequin/Silhouette Sunday Matinee Movies. These four movies are based on bestselling Harlequin and Silhouette novels.

Camera... As the cameras roll, be the first to read the original novels the movies are based on!

Action... Through this offer, you can have these books sent directly to you! Just fill in the order form below and you could be reading the books...before the movie!

48288-4	Treacherous Beauties by Cheryl Emerson	$3.99 U.S./$4.50 CAN.	☐
83305-9	Fantasy Man by Sharon Green	$3.99 U.S./$4.50 CAN.	☐
48289-2	A Change of Place by Tracy Sinclair	$3.99 U.S./$4.50CAN.	☐
83306-7	Another Woman by Margot Dalton	$3.99 U.S./$4.50 CAN.	☐

TOTAL AMOUNT $ _____
POSTAGE & HANDLING $ _____
($1.00 for one book, 50¢ for each additional)
APPLICABLE TAXES* $ _____
TOTAL PAYABLE $ _____
(check or money order—please do not send cash)

To order, complete this form and send it, along with a check or money order for the total above, payable to Harlequin Books, to: **In the U.S.:** 3010 Walden Avenue, P.O. Box 9047, Buffalo, NY 14269-9047; **In Canada:** P.O. Box 613, Fort Erie, Ontario, L2A 5X3.

Name: _____

Address: _____ City: _____

State/Prov.: _____ Zip/Postal Code: _____

*New York residents remit applicable sales taxes.
Canadian residents remit applicable GST and provincial taxes.

CBSPR

"HOORAY FOR HOLLYWOOD" SWEEPSTAKES

HERE'S HOW THE SWEEPSTAKES WORKS

OFFICIAL RULES — NO PURCHASE NECESSARY

To enter, complete an Official Entry Form or hand print on a 3" x 5" card the words "HOORAY FOR HOLLYWOOD", your name and address and mail your entry in the pre-addressed envelope (if provided) or to: "Hooray for Hollywood" Sweepstakes, P.O. Box 9076, Buffalo, NY 14269-9076 or "Hooray for Hollywood" Sweepstakes, P.O. Box 637, Fort Erie, Ontario L2A 5X3. Entries must be sent via First Class Mail and be received no later than 12/31/94. No liability is assumed for lost, late or misdirected mail.

Winners will be selected in random drawings to be conducted no later than January 31, 1995 from all eligible entries received.

Grand Prize: A 7-day/6-night trip for 2 to Los Angeles, CA including round trip air transportation from commercial airport nearest winner's residence, accommodations at the Regent Beverly Wilshire Hotel, free rental car, and $1,000 spending money. (Approximate prize value which will vary dependent upon winner's residence: $5,400.00 U.S.); 500 Second Prizes: A pair of "Hollywood Star" sunglasses (prize value: $9.95 U.S. each). Winner selection is under the supervision of D.L. Blair, Inc., an independent judging organization, whose decisions are final. Grand Prize travelers must sign and return a release of liability prior to traveling. Trip must be taken by 2/1/96 and is subject to airline schedules and accommodations availability.

Sweepstakes offer is open to residents of the U.S. (except Puerto Rico) and Canada who are 18 years of age or older, except employees and immediate family members of Harlequin Enterprises, Ltd., its affiliates, subsidiaries, and all agencies, entities or persons connected with the use, marketing or conduct of this sweepstakes. All federal, state, provincial, municipal and local laws apply. Offer void wherever prohibited by law. Taxes and/or duties are the sole responsibility of the winners. Any litigation within the province of Quebec respecting the conduct and awarding of prizes may be submitted to the Regie des loteries et courses du Quebec. All prizes will be awarded; winners will be notified by mail. No substitution of prizes are permitted. Odds of winning are dependent upon the number of eligible entries received.

Potential grand prize winner must sign and return an Affidavit of Eligibility within 30 days of notification. In the event of non-compliance within this time period, prize may be awarded to an alternate winner. Prize notification returned as undeliverable may result in the awarding of prize to an alternate winner. By acceptance of their prize, winners consent to use of their names, photographs, or likenesses for purpose of advertising, trade and promotion on behalf of Harlequin Enterprises, Ltd., without further compensation unless prohibited by law. A Canadian winner must correctly answer an arithmetical skill-testing question in order to be awarded the prize.

For a list of winners (available after 2/28/95), send a separate stamped, self-addressed envelope to: Hooray for Hollywood Sweepstakes 3252 Winners, P.O. Box 4200, Blair, NE 68009.

CBSRLS

OFFICIAL ENTRY COUPON

"Hooray for Hollywood"
SWEEPSTAKES!

Yes, I'd love to win the Grand Prize — a vacation in Hollywood —
or one of 500 pairs of "sunglasses of the stars"! Please enter me
in the sweepstakes!

This entry must be received by December 31, 1994.
Winners will be notified by January 31, 1995.

Name _____

Address _____ Apt. _____

City _____

State/Prov. _____ Zip/Postal Code _____

Daytime phone number _____
(area code)

Mail all entries to: Hooray for Hollywood Sweepstakes,
P.O. Box 9076, Buffalo, NY 14269-9076.
In Canada, mail to: Hooray for Hollywood Sweepstakes,
P.O. Box 637, Fort Erie, ON L2A 5X3.

KCH

OFFICIAL ENTRY COUPON

"Hooray for Hollywood"
SWEEPSTAKES!

Yes, I'd love to win the Grand Prize — a vacation in Hollywood —
or one of 500 pairs of "sunglasses of the stars"! Please enter me
in the sweepstakes!

This entry must be received by December 31, 1994.
Winners will be notified by January 31, 1995.

Name _____

Address _____ Apt. _____

City _____

State/Prov. _____ Zip/Postal Code _____

Daytime phone number _____
(area code)

Mail all entries to: Hooray for Hollywood Sweepstakes,
P.O. Box 9076, Buffalo, NY 14269-9076.
In Canada, mail to: Hooray for Hollywood Sweepstakes,
P.O. Box 637, Fort Erie, ON L2A 5X3.

KCH